"Absolutely amazing, easy to read, perfect romance with mystery and drama story. There were so many wonderful elements that gave twists and turns to this adventure on the sea. I absolutely loved this story and can't rave about it enough."—*LesbiReviewed*

Going Up

"This story is a refreshing light in the lesfic world. Or should I say in the romance lesfic world? Why do you ask me? Well, while there is a lot of crushy feeling between wlw characters and all, but, honestly that's the sub-plot and I've adored that fact. *Going Up* is a lesson in life."—*Kam's Queerfic Pantry*

"The author takes an improbable twosome and writes such a splendid romance that you actually think it is possible…this is a great romance and a lovely read."—*Best Lesfic Reviews*

Mergers and Acquisitions

"This book is fun, witty, and adorable. I had no idea which way this book was going to take me, and I loved it. Each character is interesting and loveable in their own right. You don't want to miss this one—heck, if you have read any of A.E. Radley's books you know it's quality stuff."—*Romantic Reader Blog*

The Startling Inaccuracy of the First Impression

"We absolutely loved the way the relationship between the two ladies developed. There is nothing hurried about the relationship that develops perfectly organically. This is a lovely, easy to read romance."—*Best Lesfic Reviews*

Huntress

"A.E. Radley always writes fantastic books. *Huntress* is a little different than most of her books, but just as wonderful. The humor was fantastic, the story was absolutely adorable, and the writing was superb. This is truly one of those books where the characters really stick with you long after the book has ended. I wish I'd read it sooner. 5 Stars." —*Les Rêveur*

Bring Holly Home

"*Bring Holly Home* is a fantastic novel and probably one of my favourite books by A.E. Radley…Such a brilliant story and one I know I will read time and time again. This book has two ingredients that I love in novels, Ice Queens melting and age-gap romance. It's definitely a slow burn but one I'd gladly enjoy rereading again."—*Les Rêveur*

Keep Holly Close

"It was great to go back into the world of the Remember Me series. The first book in the series, *Bring Holly Home*, is one of my favourite A.E. Radley books. I love Holly and Victoria; they tick all the boxes for me when it comes to my favourite tropes. Plus, Victoria's kids are adorable, especially little Alexia. She melts my heart."—*Les Rêveur*

"So much drama...loved it!!! I already loved Holly and Victoria from the first book in the series, *Bring Holly Home*, so it was brilliant to be back with them. Victoria hasn't changed and I adore her as much as before. She was utterly brilliant at every moment of this follow-up story and she even managed to surprise me from time to time. The Remember Me series is so beautiful and one of my all time favourites. 5 of 5 stars."—*LesbiReviewed*

Climbing the Ladder

"Radley has a talent for giving us memorable characters to love, women you wish you knew, and locations you wish you could experience firsthand."—*Late Night Lesbian Reads*

Second Chances

"This is an absolute delight to read. Likeable characters, well-written, easy flow and sweet romance. Definitely recommended."—*Best Lesfic Reviews*

The Road Ahead

"I really enjoyed this age-gap, opposites attract road trip romance. This is a romance where the characters actually acknowledge their differences and joy of joy, listen to each other. I love it when a book makes me feel all the feels and root for both women to find their HEA. Hilarious one minute, heart-tugging the next. A pleasure to read." —*Late Night Lesbian Reads*

Fitting In

"Writing convincing love stories with non-typical characters is tricky. Radley more than measures up to the challenge with this truly heart-warming romance."—*Best Lesfic Reviews*

By the Author

Romances

Mergers & Acquisitions

Climbing the Ladder

A Swedish Christmas Fairy Tale

Second Chances

Going Up

Lost at Sea

The Startling Inaccuracy of
the First Impression

Fitting In

Detour to Love

Under Her Influence

Protecting the Lady

Humbug

Reading Her

Reclaiming Love

Maybe, Probably

Taking the Plunge

The Flight Series

Flight SQA016

Grounded

Journey's End

The Remember Me Series

Bring Holly Home

Keep Holly Close

The Around the World Series

The Road Ahead

The Big Uneasy

Mystery Novels

Huntress

Death Before Dessert

Visit us at www.boldstrokesbooks.com

TAKING THE PLUNGE

by

Amanda Radley

2023

TAKING THE PLUNGE

ISBN 13: 978-1-63679-400-6

This Trade Paperback Original Is Published By
Bold Strokes Books, Inc.
P.O. Box 249
Valley Falls, NY 12185

First Edition: October 2023

CREDITS
Editor: Ruth Sternglantz
Production Design: Stacia Seaman
Cover Design by Amanda Radley

For the readers.

CHAPTER ONE

Regina Avery stood outside the cafe next door to her office building and considered doing something she very rarely, if ever, considered. Taking a risk. She'd been eyeing the menu's newest item, a white chocolate chai tea, several mornings in a row. She loved white chocolate but worried that the drink might be too sweet. Or that the flavours of white chocolate and chai wouldn't work together. Most of all she worried if she'd miss her usual. Would she regret changing up her routine?

In the end, she decided not to chance it. Starting the morning without her usual takeaway tea with milk and two sugars could make for a bad start to the day. There was nothing wrong with normal tea, she reminded herself. She'd always thought of it as normal tea, even if it was technically English breakfast tea. To Regina, it was simply tea. And it was her one addiction.

But despite always drinking exactly the same thing, she often looked at alternatives on menus, drawn in by the comforting photography and appealing graphic design. That was the problem with working in marketing—you noticed advertisements and product placements everywhere, probably more so than the average person.

Stepping into the cafe, she placed her usual order. If the barista pitied her ordering the same thing that she had ordered every day for years, they didn't show it. While she waited, she thought about her upcoming workday. It was going to be a light day, only a few meetings about the latest marketing campaign for their oldest client.

Regina had a great relationship with them and had come up with some promising ideas over the weekend. While she could have been resting, catching up on reading, or choosing colours for her planned redecoration of her bathroom, instead she'd researched new campaign concepts for her clients. Because that was what Regina always did. She got to know her clients and found the perfect marketing strategies for them. Even in her downtime. Especially lately.

Since her break-up a few months before, and even during the last few months of the strained relationship, she'd been taking more and more work home with her. She loved what she did, but even she was aware that she sometimes used work to ignore situations.

Tea in hand, she entered the offices of Precision Marketing. Her mind swam with the ideas she had collated over the weekend and the best way to get them all in order for the presentation later that day.

She'd only just stepped out of the lift when she could sense that something was wrong. The office was noisier than usual, and an air of something uncomfortable nipped at her. Within seconds, her assistant ran towards her.

"Have you heard?" Jenny asked, red cheeked and glassy-eyed.

"Heard what? I just got here." Regina looked over Jenny's shoulder, trying to figure out what had happened. Some of her colleagues looked worried—others looked angry.

"I thought they might've called you." Jenny shifted her weight from foot to foot. "The rumours are all over the office. Someone in the communications team has seen the press release already. I'm talking to my uncle about taking a job in his firm."

"Slow down," Regina commanded. She put her tea on the reception desk. "Tell me what's happened."

"Peter's filed for bankruptcy. Precision Marketing is over."

Regina stared at her assistant. Well, ex-assistant apparently. How could this be? It surely couldn't be true?

"Sam said that we'll all be locked out by lunchtime," Jenny continued.

Regina held up her hand to calm Jenny down. "Where is Peter?"

Jenny shrugged. "He had a meeting first thing with Christine and then he left."

Regina spun on her heel and headed towards the chief financial officer's corner office. Christine Booth had been at Precision Marketing for as long as Regina had. They'd both worked hard to grow the agency from a small player in the busy London scene to a sizable company.

Somehow, everything was falling apart. Panic built up within her. Her hard work had earned her a very good salary and regular bonuses, which she relied on, especially now that the rent on her tiny London apartment had gone up for the second time that year.

But her biggest expense, the one she could never scale back on, was the care home where her beloved aunt lived. Bess Avery was the only family Regina had left since her parents died in a ski lift accident thirty years ago. Bess had been in and out of a couple of local care homes, each with its own issues, before finally finding a place that she could call home. It was eye-wateringly expensive, but Regina would spare no cost in ensuring that Bess was happy, safe, and well.

Bess had spent her life looking after others, not only in her career as a care worker, but as guardian for a heartbroken fourteen-year-old Regina. Her independence was brought to a crushing end when she suffered a stroke a few years ago. Through a mixture of therapy and luck, Bess had bounced back for the most part, but living alone without nearby support was out of the question.

Regina's well-paying job and complete lack of a social life meant that she had plenty of disposable income and had insisted on paying for the care home, even going so far as to shield Bess from the true cost.

It meant that Regina had little in the way of savings to fall back on. Bills were coming at the end of the month, and she had no way to cover them without a job, something she hadn't even thought to worry about until a few moments ago. Her job had always felt safe to her. Precision Marketing was a strong company, and she was one of the top performing executives. The thought that she'd turn up one day and find everything gone was almost too ridiculous to believe.

She knocked on Christine's closed office door and opened it without waiting for a reply. Christine looked up in surprise but nodded in greeting when she saw who had entered.

"What's happening?" Regina got right to the point.

Christine gestured for Regina to close the door, which she did.

"Peter took out a massive loan against the company years ago," Christine explained, still typing on her keyboard as she did. "Some piece of software that he thought would be the next big thing. It was full of bugs. Practically worthless. But he threw more and more money at it so he could get it into a state to sell."

Regina folded her arms and stood in front of Christine's desk. She was furious but knew the failure lay on Peter's shoulders and not Christine's, even if it was hard to temper her anger there and then.

She glanced at the chair and remembered the countless times she had sat down, and they had talked, laughed, and cried about all manner of things over the years. A shiver ran up her spine as she realised that was all about to come to an end. Her previously secure job was about to vanish. Finding out why was important, but it wouldn't change anything.

"Turns out the software was a poor copy, code stolen from another company. They sued and won, and now we're done."

Regina opened and closed her mouth a couple of times. "But…"

"I didn't know about it either," Christine said.

"Is there anything that we can do?"

"Contact a good recruitment agency."

Regina blinked. "Surely there's something—"

"It's over," Christine said. "I've seen the figures we're looking at. No one will loan us money. Even if they did, it would bankrupt us all over again to try to pay it off. We're done, Regina. Go home—there's no point in hanging around here. I'm just getting my papers in order."

Anger radiated from Christine in thick waves, and Regina couldn't blame her. Peter had always been a bit of a maverick, but it had always worked in their favour until now.

"I'll call you tonight," Christine said. "We can meet up and talk about this over a glass of wine. But it's probably best to get out of the office—everyone's getting upset."

Regina turned and looked through the half-closed blinds. Some people were packing their belongings. Some were pacing while on phone calls. Small groups were talking and pointing towards Peter's closed office door. Regina was struck by how all of them, and all the ones who had yet to arrive in the office, were suddenly out of work, on an average Wednesday afternoon that had seemed mundane just thirty minutes ago.

It was her worst nightmare. Not losing her job, but the sudden upheaval of something that was so important in her life. The fact that life could change in an instant, through no fault of her own, sent a wave of real fear through her. She was in her mid-forties and learning, yet again, that she had no real control over her own life.

She turned back to Christine. "I'll call you later."

Christine nodded. "If you see Peter, punch him for me."

Regina nodded and left the office. She ducked her head and walked over to her own office where Jenny was standing and looking anxiously at her. Jenny, like Regina, was clearly processing what had happened and was trying to make sense of the situation and figure out next steps.

"Pack your things," Regina said. "HR will be in touch with everyone later regarding what's happened and what to expect regarding pay."

"So it's true?"

"It's true." Regina barely believed it herself.

"Wow. I'm going to have to update my CV." Jenny flopped down onto her chair and stared at her desk in disbelief. "I don't want to change job. I like it here."

"Same," Regina agreed. "Obviously, I'm happy to give you a reference. You have my private email address."

"Thank you." Jenny sighed and looked up at her. "What will you do now?"

Regina had no idea. She needed a job as fast as possible, but that wasn't easy at her level. The closer you got to the top of the career pyramid, the fewer roles were available at any one time. She often browsed corporate social media platforms and jobs boards, just out of curiosity, to see what was happening in the market. But now her mind was a blank. Panic was all she could feel, cold and almost overwhelming. She kept it at bay, knowing that people needed to see her strong right now.

"I'm not sure," she said brightly. She knew she needed to feign some kind of confidence until she was at home and able to fall apart in private. "I'll see what's out there, I suppose."

It took just five minutes for Regina to pack up her things and place them in a box that had once contained reams of paper. She said her farewells, promised to give references to anyone who needed them, and left the Precision Marketing offices for the last time.

The late-September wind was eye piercing and whipped around her neck without mercy. She mechanically flicked up the collar of her blazer. Despite the cold, she avoided the Tube station and instead started to walk home. Sitting still would unbalance her further. She needed to process what had happened and think what she might do next.

Only when she got home did she realise she had left her takeaway tea undrunk on the receptionist's desk.

Chapter Two

Regina sat at her kitchen table and stared into nothing. As soon as she'd arrived home, she'd opened her MacBook and started to write a to-do list. It hadn't been long before she'd become overwhelmed with the hopelessness of the situation and her eyes had drifted to simply stare at the far wall instead.

Living payday to payday was fine when the paydays came regularly. But knowing that the next one would be her last and would be smaller than she was accustomed was causing panic to rise within her.

Regina wasn't good with panic. It quickly swept over her, and she felt powerless to stop or slow it. Being unable to cope with unpredictable situations had kept her walking a safe path her entire life, never taking a risk, never doing anything that might fail.

But she had been wilfully blind to the financial black hole that lurked around the corner, able to suck her in at any time but kept at bay month after month by the regular pay being deposited.

She'd never been one for spending money on herself, with little interest in clothes, technology, or travel—and with no one else to spend her money on, she'd happily invested everything she had in Bess's well-being. Each month, Regina watched a large sum for Bess's care leave her bank account the very next day after she had been paid by her employer. And each month a small voice at the back of her head whispered that there was no safety net. And each time, Regina ignored it because she didn't know what the alternative was.

She didn't have a plan B. Bess needed care, and that cost money. And everything had worked so well for years—it had seemed foolish to waste time worrying about it. She told herself that there were many people who stayed in their jobs until they retired. And while Bess was in reasonably good health, she wasn't getting any younger. She'd convinced herself that there was no use worrying about a situation that would quite likely never arise.

Now she wished she had spent a little more time worrying about it. It would mean that she wasn't sitting at her kitchen table wondering what she might be able to sell in order to raise some much-needed capital.

The problem was, she didn't really have anything to sell. She rented her flat, didn't own a car, and had little of value. Regina had always been considerate before she purchased anything. The shopping bug had never bitten her, which led to a spartan life. She had everything she wanted, but nothing more. And nothing that could easily be sold.

The only solution would be to get a new job as fast as possible, which was easier said than done. At her rank, vacancies were scarce. While marketing assistants were advertised with regularity, marketing directors were few and far between.

Her eyes flicked to the job search open on her screen. There was next to nothing for someone with her experience wanting a senior role. Taking a lower-paid position was off the table. No one would hire a marketing director to do a lesser role, knowing full well that she would soon leave. Not to mention that being in a lower-paid role meant that she'd not have time to look for a job that could pay what she needed. She'd just be adding more debt to the pile.

When she'd first gotten home, she'd called a couple of recruitment consultants in the hope they'd have the ideal role waiting for her. All had said the market was quiet at the moment and confirmed her fears that there were no suitable senior openings on the books.

Each had told her to keep looking, as the right job could be posted at any time, but that didn't help to quell Regina's rising panic. One had suggested posting on LinkedIn, saying that announcing you're open to work could attract recruitment agents and internal hiring managers. But Regina felt a little too proud to do so. She never used her LinkedIn account, and popping up to tell the world that she'd lost her job and was in dire need of employment made her feel uncomfortably vulnerable.

Her mind drifted to her aunt. It had been just the two of them for a while. Bess had been beside Regina through every major event in her life, and in return Regina had decided to look after Bess in her later years. They shared everything, and Regina knew that she needed to be honest and tell Bess what had happened. Even if she didn't have all the answers yet, Bess did deserve to know if her life was about to be turned upside down.

Regina stood and walked around her one-bedroom apartment and wondered if there was any chance that they could live in the small space, even temporarily. She knew it was a pointless thought. Bess needed care that Regina could not provide.

Knowing that there was no alternative, she returned to the kitchen and closed her laptop. She swiped her blazer off the back of the chair and headed out to have the uncomfortable conversation with Bess.

❖

After a twenty-minute train journey into the London suburbs and five minutes in a taxi, Regina arrived at the Calm Acres care home. The grounds were immaculately kept and surrounded a lovingly converted Victorian school building.

Before finding Calm Acres, Regina had toured a number of nursing homes and had found most of them to be cold, austere-looking places, either so run-down they were crumbling around the residents' ears, or depressing, modern buildings that lacked any appeal.

Calm Acres had immediately felt like home. And it was one of the few places Regina could leave after a visit and not feel as if she was leaving her beloved aunt in a prison.

She took a fortifying breath of crisp, fresh air before heading up the short flight of stairs and into the main entrance. The receptionist glanced up and welcomed her with a smile and a tilt of her head, indicating that Bess was in the former library, now a games room.

In the quiet room, Bess and three other women sat around a small table, each clutching a handful of cards to her chest and eyeing the others up competitively.

"I know you have my aces," Bess told Anna.

"If I did, that would make them my aces," Anna replied, a glint in her eye.

Bess was about to reply when she looked up and saw Regina. She quickly lowered her cards face down to the table and got to her feet.

"Darling! I wasn't expecting to see you." Bess held her arms out, and Regina hurried into the embrace. "Or was I?"

Memory issues were thankfully not something Bess had experienced as she aged. But being surrounded by friends who did suffer with gaps in their recollection had left Bess worried and highly aware of the possibility.

"No, I'm just stopping by." Regina couldn't bring herself to say anything just yet. Being in her aunt's company was the soothing balm she needed after such a long and difficult morning.

"You all know my Regina," Bess said, beaming proudly as she gestured to her.

The three women all smiled and nodded.

"Pull up a chair, poppet." Bess pointed to a chair at a nearby table. "No work today?"

Regina lifted the chair and placed it next to Bess. "Not this afternoon."

"Oh, good, good. You don't want to be cooped up in an office all day," Bess said as she sat down and picked up her cards again.

"What are you playing?" Regina asked, eager for another topic of conversation. The matter of work, or lack thereof, could wait until later when they were alone. It was bad enough that she had to tell Bess that she'd lost her job—she certainly wasn't going to do that in the company of Bess's friends. While the ladies were lovely, there was something of a gossip community at Calm Acres and Regina had no intention of being its subject matter.

"Go Fish," Bess said. "But the stakes are high."

Regina swallowed nervously. "Stakes?" Now was not the time for Bess to be gambling.

"Men," Elsie, Bess's closest friend, said.

Regina raised an eyebrow. "Men?" Worries of debt gave way to the fear that her aunt and friends were somehow trading humans.

"Sort of," Elsie said. "Dates with men."

Regina looked to Bess for clarification.

"All the men keep dying off," Bess explained. "So now we're left with precious few of them while us poor women keep hanging around, getting lonelier and lonelier."

"Except the lesbians," Clara added. "They're fine."

Anna nodded. "Yes, they have each other. And we're left fighting over the men who are left. We thought we'd make it nice and fair, and we'd play for first dibs."

"This is why I keep insisting that you find someone to spend your life with, Regina," Bess said. "It's no fun to be this age and be alone."

Bess had been not so subtle over the years in encouraging Regina to find someone to settle down with. Visits to Calm Acres often included a folded-up slip of paper with a mobile telephone number of a resident's daughter, niece, or granddaughter who was a single lesbian. Regina kindly handed the numbers back, advising Bess that dating didn't work like that these days. An unsolicited call from a stranger wouldn't go down very well, even if Regina had the courage to make a call. Which she most certainly didn't.

"Yes, I know," Regina allowed. She did know. Not that she did much about it. Dating was hard, and finding someone who she wished to date harder still. She'd been either alone or in short, bad relationships for so long it was becoming normal for her to picture herself as a spinster for her entire life.

The women continued to play cards, and Regina furtively eyed her aunt. New wrinkles had appeared at her brow and where her mouth turned down. She was lonely and had been for many years. Regina had done her best to regularly visit. But she knew that only filled a few short hours here and there.

Still, at Calm Acres Bess at least had friends.

Regina's stomach ached at the idea of taking that away. As she watched them play, the strength to tell Bess about her sudden unemployment slowly wilted. She couldn't add more worry lines to the face she adored. And she couldn't allow her own bad luck and poor planning to impact her innocent aunt.

She stayed for a couple of hours, eventually being dealt in to a few hands of Go Fish and quickly realising that she was as easy to read as if she was playing with a transparent deck of cards. The upset of what had happened that day was impacting her in ways she couldn't recognise. Being unable to remember who had asked for eights was one of them.

In the end, she kissed Bess on the cheek and made her escape.

On the train home, she downloaded the LinkedIn app and logged in on her phone. She composed a message advising her connections that she was out of a job and actively looking for a new opportunity. It felt desperate and like she was begging for a job, but she reminded herself that it was all true and she needed to swallow her pride. If not for herself, then for Bess.

After a final proofread, she posted the message and closed down the app.

It would probably come to nothing, but at least she could now tell herself that she'd done everything she could.

Chapter Three

Two days later, Regina's phone lit up with an incoming call from an unknown number. Usually, she avoided unknown calls like the plague, but with desperation at a high level, she'd happily take the risk. It had been two days of searching online job forums and calling every recruitment consultant in her field to no avail. So, the incoming call was a welcome surprise that caused Regina to almost drop the phone in her hurry to answer.

"Hi there, is this Regina Avery?" the caller asked chipperly.

"It is, yes."

"Wonderful! I'm Nicole, I'm one of the recruitment managers for Amandine."

Regina immediately felt two conflicting emotions spread over her. The first was relief that someone working in recruitment was calling her. The second was frustration that she didn't have her laptop to hand and couldn't check the company name as it wasn't ringing any bells.

"Oh, hello," Regina said while she hurried to the kitchen to perform a quick Google search.

"We saw your post on LinkedIn, and your profile looks like an exact match for who we're looking for," Nicole explained.

Regina almost collapsed onto the dining room chair, her laptop briefly forgotten as relief washed over her.

"That's wonderful news," Regina said, waiting for Nicole to provide some more details.

"We're looking for an experienced marketing director to run a new department we're launching. To be perfectly honest with you, we had someone who was expected to start this week, but she had to pull out due to personal reasons. We're looking for someone to start as soon as possible as the ball is already running, so our CEO is very keen to fill this vacancy. May I ask your salary expectations?"

Regina pulled her laptop closer and opened a new browser window. In the excitement, the company name had escaped her. She told Nicole her desired salary and added that she was free to start as soon as convenient for the company, hoping that her immediate availability would seal the deal for her.

Nicole confirmed the salary was slightly above Regina's expectations and ran through the other benefits information.

"Of course, I'll send this all over to you via email so you can read through the details," Nicole said. "I know this is a little rushed."

Regina couldn't help but feel a little flustered. She'd gone from unemployed to being offered a role out of the blue. She paused. Nicole was speaking as if the role was already hers, which was extremely unusual and surely too good to be true.

"Will there be an interview?" Regina asked.

"We'd like to invite you to take on the role on a trial basis," Nicole said, "for one month, and then we can see if we're a good fit."

Regina started to realise just how desperate they must be to be offering her a job out of the blue. She was about to ask another question when Nicole spoke again.

"And, of course, we have someone here who has personally vouched for you, so I'm certain this is fate. I know that being made suddenly redundant is hard, but hopefully you'll be super happy here at Amandine."

The question of who was vouching for her disappeared at the second mention of the company name, and Regina shouldered her phone and typed the name into the search bar. She ruffled her nose at the women's fashion website that popped up in the first search spot. Regina was not a fashionista by any stretch of the imagination.

Her work outfit consisted of similar suits in similar charcoal shades, white easy-iron shirts, basic low-heeled black boots, and a black overcoat in the winter. She bought suits and all her outfits based on a comfort-first basis, definitely not something that a fashion brand would appreciate.

How was she going to develop not only an understanding but an interest in fashion? Nicole might have been sure they'd be a good match, but Regina knew for sure that they wouldn't be. She had no experience of the world of fashion, and while some marketing skills were easily transferrable, not all were.

She hesitated and wondered if she should turn the job down. It was obvious to her that she'd be extremely lucky to get through her month's probation period.

Thoughts of Bess popped into her mind. Regina worried her lip as Nicole spoke at a mile a minute about Amandine's credentials as a top-rated employer.

She couldn't turn such a gift down. She had nothing else in the pipeline, and here was a job out of the blue, right salary, starting immediately. Nerves pricked at her as she wondered if she'd be able to do enough research to make Amandine think she knew what she was doing.

It was a risk, something Regina hated, but she had little choice.

"So, what's your email address, and I'll send you over all the details," Nicole said.

Regina hesitated a moment. This was it. It was either take the job or turn it down. Now or never. She reeled off her email address and told Nicole how grateful she was for the opportunity.

Nicole seemed relieved, presumably out of a sticky situation following the previous candidate who had dropped out. A few moments later, and with scant further information, she ended the call with a faux-sounding insistence that Regina get in touch if she needed anything.

Regina lowered the phone to the table and stared into nothingness. It seemed she was now the marketing director of a new department for a fashion brand. It was nearly as frightening as being unemployed.

CHAPTER FOUR

Following the surprise telephone call, Regina read the various bits of paperwork, signed them, and returned them to Nicole. They agreed Regina would start the next week, just a few short days away.

She spent the entire weekend working her way through Amandine's website and trying to get a feel for the style and brand voice the company employed. With precious little to go on about her new role, it was the only practical thing she could think to do.

On a not-so-practical note, she worried about her work wardrobe and just how she might be able to get through her probation period. Most of all, she wondered who had personally vouched for her. Regina had worked with a number of people over the years, but she couldn't remember anyone who had ever worked in the fashion industry. And LinkedIn gave her no clues, saying that she shared no connections at all with anyone who worked at Amandine. That said, Regina had been terrible at keeping up with connections on the social media platform over the years. And she'd worked with so many people during her years in marketing agencies that the list of potential contacts was literally in the hundreds.

By the time Monday morning came around, Regina was a bag of nerves and desperate to make a good impression. She turned up at Amandine headquarters at precisely nine thirty, as requested. While the young girl on reception made all the right noises and attempted a smile, it was clear that she was visibly distraught by Regina's middle-of-the-road suit as she asked Regina to wait in the seating area for the head of marketing.

Regina had briefly considered shopping for a new outfit, but with no knowledge whatsoever to go on it would just be throwing good money away. She'd discovered that Amandine specialised in casual clothes, sleepwear, eveningwear, and swimwear. Or so it claimed on the website. The casual range wasn't at all casual to Regina's eye. It was the sort of casual an Instagram influencer spent several hours preparing. Everything was expensive, dry-clean only, and extremely on-trend.

Regina hoped that the new department would include a line of workwear, so she'd know exactly what she was expected to wear.

Perched on the edge of the sofa, she felt her nerves spark through her body. She had to get this right. Somehow, she had to convince the head of marketing that there hadn't been a giant mistake and that she could do the job. Whatever that job was.

The clicking of high heels around the corner told Regina that someone was arriving, probably her future boss.

"Ah, there you are," the newcomer said, coming into view.

Regina's stomach dropped.

She knew the voice before she'd even finished turning to greet the woman. She hoped she was wrong, but a glance at the tall woman in her trademark black dress told her that it was indeed her ex, Margot.

Just over six months ago she had ripped herself away from the toxic relationship with a promise to never get caught up in Margot's web again.

Margot stood with all the casual cockiness of someone who had been dumped and managed to exact a terrible revenge on their ex. Her arms were folded and a smirk graced her harsh features, features which Regina felt had changed since they'd last seen one another. She wondered if Margot had been under the knife for one of the cosmetic procedures she would constantly talk about. If she had, Regina wasn't sure it had gone well. Not that she was an expert in such things.

Regina had always thought Margot rather pretty to look at. They'd met a few times at work gatherings when clients had been invited to the local pub following a successful campaign launch. Regina had shyly looked at Margot with no intention of doing anything more.

Margot was full of confidence and had asked Regina out. They'd dated for a few months before…Well, it wasn't something Regina wanted to repeat. In fact, seeing Margot again at all wasn't something Regina had wanted to repeat.

Regina slowly stood up. It was obvious in that second that Margot was the person who had vouched for her.

"Welcome to Amandine," Margot said. "I took on the head of marketing role six months ago, and when I saw your sorry little post on LinkedIn, I had to have you."

Regina swallowed nervously. "You're the…"

"Head of marketing? Yes. And this new role reports directly to me."

"But we're not connected on LinkedIn," Regina noted. She remembered blocking Margot after the break-up from hell. She might not have logged in often, but cutting all ties with the woman was high on her priority list at the time.

"Not on my usual account," Margot confessed, a slight smirk indicating some stalking through a dummy account was at play.

"Why me?" Regina asked. Their break-up had been hard for both of them, but with Regina the instigator, it had been Margot who had taken it the hardest. "You said you never wanted to see me again, remember?"

Margot's expression soured. Regina flashbacked to the times when she'd seen that very look and had known that their relationship was doomed.

On paper, they looked like a good fit. They had similar backgrounds, were both in their mid-forties, worked in similar fields, and both enjoyed quiet weekends going for walks in the city and visiting museums.

In reality, they were not a good match at all. Margot was

clingy and demanding. At first, the clingy behaviour had been cute, but when it morphed into possessiveness, Regina didn't find it so endearing. The more Regina pulled away, the closer Margot tried to pull her. Tantrums and bouts of silent treatment became normal, and Regina knew she had to be the one to break things off.

Margot didn't take the break-up well, declaring that no one had ever broken up with her before and Regina was wrong to do so. If Regina had needed any further confirmation that she was doing the right thing, that was it.

"Business comes first," Margot ground out.

Regina didn't believe her for a moment. There was a cat that got the cream look to Margot that made Regina shiver.

"I knew you'd be perfect for the job," Margot continued. "Can't be easy, being made redundant so suddenly, not with those care home bills you have to shoulder."

Regina kept her mouth clamped shut. Margot was trying to push her buttons, but there was no way she'd be given the satisfaction by Regina.

"I told the CEO that you'd be ready to hit the ground running— she's very keen to see you in action. I can go into more detail later, but you're needed now at the shoot. No time to waste."

Margot turned and stalked away, Regina quickly falling into step beside her.

"The photographers need constant hand-holding, otherwise they go off script and get too artsy. We need things done the Amandine way. I presume you've reviewed our website?"

"I have," Regina confirmed.

Margot swiped her access card, and they left reception and made their way through the offices at a quick pace.

"HR suggested I pair you with an experienced assistant," Margot said, "to help you settle in."

Regina detected a hint of irritation in her tone and wondered if Margot's plan was to embarrass Regina by watching her fail. Or worse, rescue her from the edge of failure and expect some kind of gratitude.

"Arjun has been at Amandine for three years." Margot stopped by a desk and gestured to the man in his mid-twenties. "And your office is there." Margot gestured to a room hidden behind a row of filing cabinets. A clear snub.

Arjun stood up and held out his hand to Regina. "Hi, great to meet you."

Regina shook his hand. "Likewise, I'm looking forward to working together."

"No time to waste," Margot said, already walking on. "Arjun, give Regina the Amandine photographic brand guideline book I asked you to prepare."

Arjun handed Regina an inch-thick book with an apologetic look.

Regina spent a moment gaping at the book and wondering how she'd get through it while there was a photo shoot apparently in progress. She shook her head and hurried after Margot.

"We have our own studios, so much easier that way," Margot explained. "When we're not having shoots, we rent the space out to others. But with the new launch, we're in the middle of a large schedule of shoots."

A few corridors later and they approached what appeared to be a series of studios. Margot opened the double doors, and they both entered the room. It was dark by the doorway with all the light focused on the opposite wall where two grey sofas were set up and a photographer was adjusting his lighting equipment.

"Oh yes," Margot said, snapping her fingers as if suddenly remembering an important point. "I did forget to mention. This role oversees the launch of our new range. There's a lot riding on this. I'm sure you can manage, but if you can't and I have to step in… Well, let's say that it won't look good. Especially as I've already sent out the press release about your starting here to every marketing and business publication."

Regina ground her teeth. This was a set-up. This was Margot's way to get back at her. With her name now being associated to Amandine, leaving in a short period of time would look terrible.

A door on the other side of the room opened, and five women in long dressing gowns entered the room, all chatting and giggling as they did.

Margot stood very close to Regina. "One more thing, I probably should have mentioned this sooner, but the new range is for women's lingerie."

As if on cue, the women dispensed with their dressing gowns. Regina saw quick flashes of silk and lace in pale pastels before she slammed her eyes shut. She felt her breath restrict and her cheeks heat up.

Margot chuckled under her breath. "Oh dear. I completely forgot—you have a bit of an issue with all this, don't you? Well, now's the time to get over that."

Of course Margot hadn't forgotten Regina's very real discomfort when it came to nudity. She wasn't a prude, but for some completely unfathomable reason an overwhelming feeling of mortifying embarrassment would shoot through her whenever she saw something provocatively sexual, like lingerie. She'd never been able to understand why, or to shake it, but from short shorts to burlesque shows, Regina was out of her depth. Her complexion would light up like a traffic stop sign, and she'd find it impossible to make eye contact.

"The CEO is looking for lingerie to be one of our anchor brands within three years. There's going to be a lot of attention on this new range. It's good, too. The cut, the fabric, the styling. It's just going to be about cutting through the noise of our competitors and letting people see that Amandine belongs in this space. The marketing will really be make or break here," Margot explained. "So whatever silly little issue you have with seeing a bit of flesh, well, you better get over it. Fast."

Regina turned around and opened her eyes if only to glare daggers at Margot. Margot knew full well that Regina couldn't simply get over it. It had been a lifelong issue that Regina had been powerless to overcome.

Margot leaned in close. "The entire marketing industry knows you're working here, Regina. I've made sure of it. And I've made a very big deal of how you're going to be completely responsible for the success, or failure, of this very expensive launch. When it goes wrong, and it will because you can't even *look* at a model, I'll get to step in and rescue the company. Unless you want to come to an arrangement now?"

Regina opened her mouth but was silenced by Margot's finger over her lips.

"Don't make rash decisions. Think about it." Margot took a step back. "Good luck with your new job." She turned towards the photographer and raised her voice. "This is Regina Avery, your new marketing director. She'll be in charge from now on. Best of luck, everyone!"

Chapter Five

Regina sucked in a deep breath. Discomfort like she had never known it washed over her. Her unfortunate Achilles heel was going to be the end of her job and maybe even her career if Margot had anything to do with it.

Not for the first time, she cursed the unwanted embarrassment that had ailed her for as long as she could remember. It was a bizarre and persistent issue that had appeared from nowhere and held on to her with a vice-like grip. Trying to get over it had always seemed impossible, and so she'd learned to live with it, not making eye contact with lovers, avoiding looking at fellow bathers on beach holidays, and definitely not looking at lingerie models.

"Regina!" Margot snapped.

She turned to see Margot standing by a clothing rack.

The desire to walk out was strong. Margot had seen her pleading LinkedIn message and plotted a despicable type of revenge, which put Regina in a terrible predicament—face a lifelong fear head-on or be known as the marketing expert who failed to launch a new line for Amandine.

You can do this, she thought. *Somehow, you can muddle through until a time when moving on to another role is reasonable.*

She allowed her gaze to leave Margot and the clothing rail and drift towards the models. As expected, they were stunning and the sort of women who would easily snag everyone's gaze. Regina tried to focus on their faces but soon felt the heat on her cheek.

"If you can't do this, let me know now." Margot was suddenly by her side and whispering in her ear. Her tone carried a hint of malice that convinced Regina she needed to prove Margot wrong.

"I'm fine," she lied. She pointed to the clothing rack. "What did you want to show me?"

"You're fine?" Margot threw her head back and laughed. "Come now. I know you, Regina."

"I've been getting help. I'm much better. I was just thrown by the situation, as I'm sure was your intention. But now we're all here, let's get on with things. You wanted to show me the range, I'm presuming?"

Margot's smirk waned, and Regina felt a small bit of power transferring between them.

"It's absurd, you know," Margot rallied quickly. "A forty-four-year-old woman who has dated women her entire life, actually blushing at the sight of some vapid Barbie lookalikes in knickers."

Regina was about to reply when she realised one of the models was approaching them. She wore an item of lingerie that Regina couldn't identify—if pressed, she'd call it a teddy. She made a mental note to do some research before she made a complete fool of herself with her lack of knowledge.

"Hi," the model said.

Regina looked up. She blinked and found that she was incapable of speech. The young woman was easily the most beautiful person Regina had ever seen. She had dark rose-coloured lips, a smooth almost golden complexion, masses of wavy dark brown hair that spilled over her athletic shoulders, and a pair of soulful brown eyes.

Margot did nothing to keep the irritation from her features. "Grace, this is Regina Avery. Regina, this is one of our models, Grace Holland."

"Hi," Regina said, happy that her voice seemed to manage to hold for the single syllable.

"Hey. I was just wondering if we're getting started soon or if I have time to head out for some bubble tea?"

Regina watched in amazement as Grace casually leaned against a pillar, not at all self-conscious that she was wearing nothing more than flimsy silk.

"We're starting soon," Margot said dismissively.

"The lighting isn't properly warmed up yet," Grace continued. "It will take another ten minutes, and I can get to the shop downstairs and back in less than five. This call came in last minute, so I didn't have time for breakfast. There's hardly anything to drink in the green room and I'm thirsty. Not to mention caffeine deprived."

Grace Holland wasn't what Regina had expected in a model. She'd assumed they were all quiet, meek, and nil by mouth. Grace was quickly shattering all those assumptions. After braving a further glance at Grace and the other models, she realised that Grace was a little older than the others, possibly in her early thirties. Regina wondered if that maturity gave her the courage to stand toe to toe with Margot.

Sensing an opportunity to leave the room and get some much-needed breathing space, Regina spoke up. "I'll go. I've no idea what bubble tea actually is. I've seen posters, but never tried it." She paused, realising she was starting down an avenue where she could sound like a fool. "What I'm trying to say is, with instructions, I can get that for you."

"No, Regina," Margot blurted out. "You're not an assistant." She turned to Grace. "I'll see if I can find someone. Go back on set, and I'll send someone over."

Grace looked at Margot for a beat before shrugging her shoulders and turning around, clearly not believing Margot's words.

"She's the talent—shouldn't we be getting her what she wants?" Regina asked.

"Absolutely not. It's typical model behaviour, thinking everyone should cater to their every whim. If she wants bubble tea, then she'll have to get out of bed earlier," Margot said.

"She said the call from us came in last minute," Regina pressed. It was sounding more and more like Margot was treating employees in the same way she did her partner by ruling over them.

Margot sighed. "This entire shoot has been a nightmare. If

people could just pull together, then we could get this first day behind us."

Regina glanced over to Grace, who was now talking with the other models but appeared to be holding on to the back of the sofa to keep her balance. Regina could recognise a blood sugar drop when she saw one.

"Come along, I have a meeting in ten minutes and want to get you and the photographer up to speed before that," Margot said. "We need to get aligned on the vibe we're going for, and make sure we have the right schedule. It's taken weeks to get this organised, and I don't want to miss anything."

She marched off, not checking that Regina was following her as she stalked across the room. Regina wasn't following her as she noticed Arjun entering the room and instead made her way to speak with him.

"Arjun, not to start off by sending you on errands, but could you do something for me? It won't take long."

"Of course. What do you need?"

Regina got her bank card from the compartment in her phone holder. "Here. Please go and speak to the models and ask if they want anything from the cafe downstairs, which apparently does bubble tea."

He took the card. "Sure, no problem. I know the place. It does great boba."

Regina paused for a moment, wondering if she should ask what boba was or if she should just add it to the number of things that she'd be looking up online throughout the day.

"Perfect, get yourself something, of course."

"Thanks, do you want something?"

Regina paused for a moment. She'd been so turned around by the strange day, she'd not even considered the fact that her usual order would probably help to settle her.

"Please, black tea, milk, and two sugars. Thank you so much."

If Arjun was going to say anything about the unfashionable addition of sugar to her drink, he swallowed it down. "No problem, it's what I'm here for."

Regina watched him head over towards the models. A smile with enough power to light up the night sky appeared on Grace's face as he took her drink order. She looked at Regina and mouthed a silent *thank you*.

Regina quickly looked away and followed after Margot, hoping that the blush she felt on her cheeks wasn't too visible.

CHAPTER SIX

Just two hours later the first stage of the photo shoot was over, and everyone broke for lunch. Regina was pleasantly surprised by how well she'd eventually managed to perform. Once she'd ushered Margot out of the room and acquainted herself with the brief, she'd sat behind the photographer, an overly artsy type called Thomas, and guided him through the requirements sheet.

It was a little more involved than Regina had initially thought, with photography required for magazine advertisements, a printed brochure, and the website, including close-ups of every product. With at least twenty pieces per collection, and seven collections, she quickly realised that she'd be managing photo shoots for longer than she'd initially hoped.

Thankfully, her experience was kicking in, and she was working through her list and calculating which images could be used for each medium and marking up which would need extra editing work in post-production as she went. It might have been her first lingerie shoot, but it wasn't her first product shoot. As long as she could pretend the models were the latest laptop, or a new car, she'd be fine.

"I still think a gradient fade would make this stand out," Thomas repeated as he thrust the camera into her face.

"Not in the brand guidelines," Regina said, without looking at the screen. "Sorry."

Thankfully, Thomas was so involved in his work he hadn't noticed Regina's reluctance to look at any of the images he'd captured. Yet. She knew she had a limited amount of time before someone noticed. A marketing director leading a shoot and not able to look at any of the shots wouldn't go unnoticed for long, but that was a bridge she'd cross when she got to it.

"Sometimes we have to break the rules to make art," he said.

Regina nodded. "Sometimes. But not on my first day in a new company who have provided me with a very thick and very detailed brand book. Let's stick with what we've been asked to do."

Margot had warned her that the photographers were difficult to work with, but Thomas was simply pushing against boundaries as any artist would do. That aside, he was competent and was making the photo shoot a relatively painless process.

As long as Regina didn't have to look at the models or the photos.

He handed her the camera, seemingly willing to allow the expensive piece of equipment to drop if she didn't take hold of it.

"I'm going to grab a sandwich. You look at that and tell me it wouldn't be a hundred times better with a gradient fade."

He walked away towards the green room where lunch had been set up, leaving Regina with the camera. On the screen was one of the images she'd been studiously attempting to avoid.

She wanted to drop the camera and leave. To run to the nearest bathroom, splash cold water on her face, and take some deep breaths. She glanced around the room. Some people were in the green room, but some had remained on set. Two of the models were chatting with the make-up and clothing assistants.

Regina had deliberately stayed behind the camera, knowing that she looked enrapt in work. But with Thomas gone and her holding the camera, it would be obvious that she was avoiding people unless she looked like she was working. She had to look as if she was knowledgeably checking the images on the camera screen, which was the last thing she wanted to do but marginally preferrable to mingling with semi-nude women in the green room.

She glanced down at the screen. It was an image of Grace Holland, seductively smiling as if she'd just shared a joke with a lover. She was resting a hand on her chest, right above the swell of her left breast in that rosy teddy that was somehow seared into

Regina's memory from a split-second glance. Her smile looked so genuine that her eyes even seemed to twinkle.

"That's a pretty good one. Although, if I was a little to the left, you'd see more of the lacework on the leg. I think that really makes this garment stand out. Don't you?"

Regina nearly dropped the camera at being caught looking at the image of Grace by the woman herself, something which she logically knew she was supposed to be doing. But it still somehow felt wrong to her. Like being caught peeping through a window.

"Y-yes," she agreed. "Yes, it does."

Grace smiled. "I wanted to thank you for getting us something to eat and drink. And to say that I don't make a habit of showing up to work in that state. It was just an early morning when the call came in, and I didn't have a lot of time."

"It's, um, that's fine," Regina croaked. "It sounds like it was our fault and not yours. I apologise for Margot."

Luckily, Grace wore a thick fleecy robe, so Regina could almost look at her as long as she didn't think too long about what she knew was underneath. Although looking at Grace was still tricky. Her hair lay in perfect waves around her shoulders. She was the most naturally beautiful person Regina thought she had ever seen.

But this Grace in front of her looked casual in comparison to the sexy image on the screen. In person, Grace in her robe looked relaxed and calm. Without the full face of make-up she could look as though she were having a casual Sunday morning at home. Regina quickly realised modelling work included some acting talent, with Grace able to turn some sort of character on and off at a moment's notice.

Regina hoped she was managing to look and sound like a normal person doing normal work things, even if her heart was drumming so fast it was almost making her dizzy.

"No problem. I've"—Grace seemed to be weighing her words—"worked with Margot around before."

"I'm sorry to hear that," Regina said honestly.

Grace laughed a little. "Yes, she's…interesting."

Regina wasn't about to argue. Margot was interesting,

terrifyingly so at times. Thankfully, Regina's interest had long ago waned.

"Marissa was talking about putting my hair up for the next sequence," Grace said. "Or I'll be sweeping it behind my shoulder for the close-ups of the straps. But if we do that, we'd need some extra shots so the internet product close-ups all match up. What do you think?"

Regina felt her heart start beating impossibly faster. She was starting to feel a little overheated, and she knew from experience that breathlessness was on the way, something she couldn't possibly cover up.

Grace took the camera from Regina's hand and cycled through a couple of shots. "Just from here through to the next group shot, shouldn't take long." She handed the camera back to Regina. She glanced at the screen and almost gasped at the close-up of Grace's chest.

She reminded herself that it was simply a shot to show the stitching and design of the garment, but that didn't help, and she felt as if she might faint.

"Whoa, are you okay?" Grace took the camera before Regina dropped it and clipped it back onto the tripod. She turned back to Regina and put a hand on her arm. It was supposed to steady her, but it only made Regina's heart beat faster.

"I…" Any thought of an appropriate lie vanished because of her dizziness. In her panic, her eyes darted around the room. As they landed on the camera screen, she groaned and squeezed her eyes closed.

She heard Grace crouch down beside her chair. "Regina? Are you okay? What's wrong?"

Regina lowered her head and opened her eyes. "Yes. I just need…some time. I'm sorry."

Grace made no move to leave. Instead, she worried her lip and looked around the area as she pieced the clues together. "Do you… struggle with nudity?"

Regina didn't respond but worried that her burning cheeks answered for her. She hated the way her pale skin flared up at the first sign of an embarrassing situation. And not some attractive pinking, no, it was blotchy red marks that spread over her cheeks and down her throat. And the thought that she was in her mid-forties and blushing like a schoolgirl just made the whole situation so much worse.

"Hey, it's okay," Grace said gently. "A lot of people have to get used to seeing half-naked people in their workplace. It's not an everyday thing for most people. Unless it's something to do with the same-sex touching? Because if that's the issue then I'm out of here."

Regina looked up in horror. "What? No. No, it's not that at all. I'm a lesbian."

"Oh. Good." Grace nodded. "You'd be surprised at how many people I've worked with who have an issue with that side of things."

"No. It's certainly not that." Regina hated that Grace had guessed her issue so easily. And especially hated that it was Grace, who she already had the beginnings of an inappropriate crush on.

But now that she'd started to open up, she might as well continue. "It's…nudity in general. Always has been. And I suppose it doesn't help that I am gay and really don't want any undressed women to feel, I don't know, objectified? But that's not the main issue. I've always been like this. I don't know why. It's ridiculous."

"Not at all. Are your parents the same?" Grace asked.

"Maybe they were a little. But I suffer far worse."

"Would you say that you struggle with nudity, even though you know that fear is irrational?"

"Yes." Regina didn't know what Grace was getting at, but she hoped the line of questioning might come to an end soon.

"Sounds like gymnophobia," Grace said. "It's not as uncommon as you might think."

Regina looked at Grace. "Gym-what?"

"Gymnophobia. Gymno comes from the Greek for naked. And phobia, well, you know. Haven't you heard of it? You sound like a classic case."

Regina shook her head. "No. I've never looked it up. I'm a head firmly in the sand sort of person. How do you know of it?"

"Degree in psychology." Grace shrugged. "Not using it to its full potential, but it comes in handy. I take it you've never tried to—"

Regina shook her head. "No. Nothing."

"Hm." Grace scratched the back of her neck. "It's going to be an issue in your job here at Amandine."

"Yes," Regina groaned. "And I need this job."

"Okay. Well, everything has a solution," Grace said cheerfully.

Regina sighed and shook her head. "That's not been my experience, and no offence here, but I've been around for longer than you."

"Not that much longer, surely. I'm thirty-one, which is close to retirement age in model years. I'm basically a relic."

"Well, I have thirteen years on you, and I can tell you that I don't think there's a solution to this."

Grace was quiet for a while. "I'm sure exposure therapy would work."

Regina looked at her hand in her lap and was relieved to see it wasn't shaking any more. "Isn't that where you take a person who is scared of heights to the ledge of a skyscraper roof?"

Grace chuckled. "Sort of. But a little at a time, to build up. A friend of mine had an intense phobia of the dentist. Her therapist made her talk to the dentist on the phone and get to know him. Then look at pictures of the dental surgery. Then go and sit in the waiting room. Then talk face to face to the dentist. And then, sit in the dentist's chair."

"And that worked?"

"Yes. But it took months. Working here will be some sort of exposure therapy, I guess. If that helps?"

Regina sighed. "I wonder if I should just quit now."

Her initial strength and desire to face down Margot's blackmail had almost vanished once Regina was faced with the reality of her day job. Being unemployed suddenly didn't seem so bad. Sitting at home in a dark room, on her own, seemed like bliss. Of course, she knew she'd regret it the second she walked out.

"Why did you take this job?" Grace asked.

"I was sort of pushed into it," Regina said.

Grace nodded, understanding that Regina was stuck but not willing to explain why.

"Well, one day at a time," Grace said. "Maybe I can help you? I have nearly fifteen years of experience in this business, and I have no problem looking at naked women with a detached eye, including myself. Why don't we look at some of the pictures together? If it gets too much for you, we can take a break. Or I can tell you what I think, and you can pass that off as your own opinion. If you like?"

"I can't do that. I would be claiming credit for your work."

"No, you'd be allowing one of the models to stick her nose in where it doesn't belong and start spouting her opinions. Trust me, people hate when I do that. You'd be doing me a favour."

"I think you're doing me a much bigger favour, but I'm not too proud to accept help. If you're serious about helping me?"

"Absolutely. I'd love to." Grace pulled up a chair and sat beside Regina. She picked up the shoot list and flipped through the paperwork. "Oh, you've already started thinking about the group shot post-prod work, that's great."

Regina shuffled in her seat. "I am a professional when not hampered by stunning, semi-naked women everywhere. I'm normally good at what I do. This isn't me at all."

"Glad to hear it." Grace grinned.

They'd been working through the shoot list for five minutes, making notes about what was needed, when Thomas returned. He had a sandwich in one hand and his phone in the other.

"Margot's called me up to her office for an urgent chat," he said.

"Of course she did," Regina said, wondering how much sabotaging Margot was planning to do.

"She seems in a weird mood today," Thomas said. "I'll be back as soon as I can."

During the discussion, Grace had busied herself with one of the screens, and Regina wondered if the astute young woman had guessed that Regina was the reason for Margot's sudden mood swing.

"I'm not sure about this sequence," Grace said, scrolling

through a series of three images. "I'm not surprised Thomas added these—he wants to be a bit edgy and almost combative. But these colours are romantic, not angry. I think people will want to see smiles, not this lack of emotion."

Regina had thought the exact same thing when Thomas had been directing the short sequence of shots. She'd allowed it, not wanting to cause upset and knowing she could always discard them later. It was interesting that Grace had immediately picked up on the same thing and told Regina she was on the right track.

"I completely agree. It's not the mood we're looking for. Sometimes you have to keep the photographer happy, but we won't be using them."

Grace beamed. "I'm glad we agree."

"You definitely know what you're talking about," Regina said.

Grace shrugged. "I'm a fast learner. And I've picked up a thing or two about marketing lingerie over the years. Have you worked with fashion before?"

"Never."

"But you're able to use your marketing knowledge here?" Grace asked, seemingly genuinely interested.

"For the most part. A lot of marketing knowledge is transferrable."

Grace bit her lower lip. "That's interesting. I've often wondered if marketing might be an interesting fallback career for me. I've always kept my ears and eyes open while on photo shoots. And as I said before, I like to stick my nose in everywhere anyway."

"Good for you. Curiosity breeds knowledge."

"I doubt I'll get anywhere. It's not like I have any real experience. And who'd hire a former model? We don't exactly have a reputation for being that smart." Grace turned back to the screen.

Regina looked at her profile. It struck her that someone so confident in their body could doubt themselves. "You clearly have a lot to offer any employer."

"I think I have a lot to learn. And I have no idea how to learn it."

Regina bit her lip as she mulled over an idea. It was probably a terrible plan, but she needed help and Grace seemed willing to provide it.

"How about an exchange? You help me with these photo shoot images and teach me about lingerie marketing, and I'll teach you about marketing as a whole. Does that seem like a fair exchange?"

Grace's eyes lit up. "Yes, yes! That would be amazing. But we can't do it here. Some of the girls get jealous—they think I'm trying to hog the limelight when I'm chatting with the photographer or the shoot director. But I'm just trying to manage my exit from the industry. Not that they know that."

"My office is out of the way. We could meet there," Regina suggested.

Arjun had already explained that being on the ground floor was unusual for a director. Margot was up on the fourth floor and was rarely seen slumming it with the mortals. It made sense that Margot wanted an office out of the way to keep Regina in her place and highlight just how little Margot thought of her.

"That sounds great. I'd really appreciate that. I could come and see you this afternoon. This shoot is due to finish at three."

"Sounds great. Oh, and Grace, I'd appreciate it if you don't tell anyone about my…weakness."

"Of course not. I would never do something like that," Grace promised. "Especially as you get to choose which models work with Amandine."

"I'd never—"

Grace held up her hand. "I know, sorry, that was a clumsy way of saying that you have as much power as me in this. I won't tell anyone. I promise. I better get back over there—I can see some of the girls are watching me."

Regina looked up and could see at least one of the models was frowning grumpily in Grace's direction. Regina had been so enrapt in Grace's company, she had almost forgotten they were around other people.

Grace stood up and turned to walk back to the set when she

tripped over the trailing belt of her dressing gown. Luckily, Regina was close enough to be able to reach out a hand and steady Grace by grabbing her forearm.

The touch, even though it was padded by a thick layer of fluffy fleece, made Regina's breath hitch.

Grace regained her balance. "Sorry, I can be so clumsy at times. Which is a terrible thing for a model. We're meant to be graceful and certainly not have bruises on our legs where we've bumped into stuff."

"Well, I'm glad to note that you're human like the rest of us."

"Please don't say that," Grace said, suddenly very serious. "I hate the idea that just because you're privileged enough to be born conventionally attractive that you're different than other humans. I'm just like you, but without your professional skill and the respect you get for what you can do and what you've achieved, not for some fluke of genetics. Not that modelling isn't a complicated skill in itself, but people don't see that. People see a face and a body, nothing else. Certainly no brain."

Taken aback by this clearly raw nerve she'd accidently touched, Regina said, "You definitely have a brain. I've seen that in the few moments we've spent together."

Grace smiled. "Thank you. I'm sorry. It's a sensitive subject. It's hard sometimes, being treated like a thing. Especially when you're coming to the end of your modelling career and have to show that you really do have other skills."

"Then I'm very happy to be able to help you with those other skills," Regina said.

Grace's face lit up with gratitude. "It's a date."

Then, she carried on walking towards the set, and Regina reminded herself to breathe. She really wished Grace wouldn't have used the word *date*. Her stomach fluttered again, but this time it wasn't because of any nudity.

CHAPTER SEVEN

Regina entered her office for the first time since arriving at work and was pleasantly surprised. She'd felt certain that Margot would have her sitting on an old crate and working on a laptop from the nineties. Instead, the room was furnished in the same way as the rest of the Amandine office—white, minimalist, and stylish.

She didn't hate it. But she was aware that the smallest personalisation would stick out a mile, probably by design. The office was a blank canvas for the budding artists to adorn and be seen by all.

"Hi, are you finding everything okay?" Arjun asked, entering the office and ready to jump to any task she assigned him. She still missed Jenny from Precision Marketing, but she had to admit that Arjun seemed to be leagues ahead of her former assistant.

"Everything seems to be in order," Regina said.

"You have a redecoration budget and also access to the Amandine collection in framed posters," he explained. "Let me know if you want to see the catalogue."

"Thank you." She took a seat at her desk and turned on her MacBook. IT had already been by and set up her workspace, leaving a Post-it Note with her username and password.

"Would you like me to go to the cafe downstairs and get some tea for your meeting with Grace?" Arjun offered. "I know she's a big fan of bubble tea."

Regina still wasn't entirely sure what bubble tea was, but the thought of pleasing Grace with her favourite beverage was appealing.

"If you wouldn't mind?" she asked, not wanting Arjun to think she was the sort of boss who needed him to run minor errands. She was perfectly capable of getting her own lunch—it was just that time was rushing by on her first day.

"Not a problem, hot tea for you? Same as before?"

She nodded and with that he was gone, eagerly rushing off. Definitely better than Jenny.

She glanced at the clock on her laptop screen and nervously realised that Grace would be arriving in less than fifteen minutes. She wondered again if she was making the right decision in asking Grace's advice. It was clear Grace knew far more than Regina did when it came to lingerie marketing, not to mention that she could look at the results of the photo shoot without feeling as though she was about to collapse into a panic attack.

Grace also knew Regina's deepest, darkest secret, something she had never willingly told anyone. It was something only known by others who had noticed her reaction. Never having spoken about it, she didn't even have a name for it until now. Knowing that it was a named phobia at least meant she wasn't alone in suffering from the embarrassing condition.

For some reason, Regina trusted Grace with her secret in a way she had never done with anyone else. She'd tried to hide her situation from everyone, even lovers, in the past. Now she'd spilled the beans to someone in a matter of minutes.

With no way to put the genie back in the lamp, she knew she had to carry on and hope that Grace was as trustworthy as she seemed.

Shaking her head to stop the indecision, she opened her email and browsed through the few items she had received, mainly welcome emails from the HR team, several from Margot, and one at the very top of her inbox from Thomas containing a link to the photographs from the shoot that day.

She needed to get back to him with feedback by the end of the day so he could prep for the next shoot and know what they had in the bag, and what needed to be revisited. Which meant she had to go through all the photos and be sure they were what she needed. Which definitely meant looking at them.

Suddenly, having Grace come and help her seemed like the best of ideas. There was no way she could do this alone.

When Arjun returned, he handed Regina a paper takeout mug and placed a see-through plastic cup on the desk. She thanked him before staring at the plastic cup and its strange contents of milky brown liquid with dark brown balls filling the bottom. It didn't look edible. The large straw indicated that the weird gelatinous balls were meant to be consumed, and Regina felt a little nauseous at the thought. She sipped her own tea, enjoying the bolt of hot, sugary liquid.

There was a knock on her door and Regina called, "Come in."

Grace Holland did just that. She wore a white shirt with jeans and an oversized cardigan in dark grey. Somehow, she made it look both everyday cosy but also fashionable, which Regina thought a little unfair as she knew in a similar outfit she would look as if she'd made zero effort at all. Her hair was up in some sort of elaborate updo with hairpins sparkling in the light from the spots in the ceiling.

Regina gestured to the chair in front of her desk and pushed the bubble tea towards her. "Arjun picked this up for you."

"Yes, he just told me it was the Assam chocolate milk one. I've been looking forward to trying this."

Regina felt a quick flash of jealousy but pushed it down as far as it would go. Arjun was allowed to speak to Grace—hell, he was allowed to do whatever he liked. And Regina had no hold over Grace to warrant such jealousy. She knew it meant her crush was already in full flow, and she would need to curb it.

"Thanks for this," Grace said. "I mean, letting me help. I'm really excited to be seeing this side of things and getting some more experience."

"I should be thanking you," Regina pointed out.

"Are you ready to look at the rest of the pictures?" Grace took a long sip of tea.

Regina sighed. "Not really, but here we go." She turned the laptop around so they could both see it from a sideways angle.

Grace shook her head. "That won't work—we need to be sitting on the same side to make sure we can really see properly." She stood up and dragged her chair around the table to sit beside Regina.

Seeing the tiny thumbnails of Grace and the other models in a state of undress and suddenly having Grace sit beside her, so close she could smell her perfume, made Regina instantly feel five degrees warmer. She desperately wished she could get herself under control. She felt as if a part of her was objectifying Grace in some way, when nothing could be further from the truth.

Grace opened up the photos and started scanning through them.

"Ah"—Grace tapped the screen with her finger—"this is what I was worried about. While you can see the lacework better in this shoot, don't you think it's a little bit on the erotic side? This campaign is meant to be romantic, but this angle is a little low. It looks like it's a leer travelling up the legs. Don't you think?"

Regina tried to speak. She really did. What came out was more like a squeak.

Grace's eyes widened as she realised what she had done. "Okay, I'm sorry. That was a bad picture and question to start with. Let's file that one for later."

Grace minimised the picture and scrolled through the options to pull up another. This was a casual group shot of all the models smiling and laughing. It was clear they were wearing lingerie, but the space around them provided a level of distance that Regina needed.

Grace started talking about anchor shots, the ones that were used again and again for billboards and centre magazine spreads. Lately, the market had been tipping away from a close-up of a single product and towards a line of products to show choice, she explained.

"Not just choice," Regina added, "also lifestyle."

Grace frowned. "What do you mean?"

"There are very few products that people actually need—most are simply desirable. One of the marketing tactics to get people to want to buy something that they don't need is to get them to buy into the lifestyle that goes along with it. We don't show a cycle helmet in isolation, we show it on a rugged, healthy-looking man, who is on his bike, in a beautiful forest, with all the right gear, and having the best time. Consumers are aware that we're selling them a cycle helmet, but they fall in love with the lifestyle."

"That makes a lot of sense. I always thought it was to show the whole range," Grace said.

"That's definitely a part of it. But look here"—Regina pointed to the screen—"this is a group of young, attractive women who look like they are friends, sharing a joke about something. Consumers will react to this and think *I want to be like that*."

"So this would really be a great anchor shot, then. Shall we go through and look for discards?"

Regina knew that looking for images to be discarded was an important early step. But going through all the images and looking for focus issues, light flares, or a model blinking was not something she was looking forward to.

"Probably wise," she said.

They evaluated picture after picture, archiving anything that didn't meet technical standards or had some other kind of issue that meant it couldn't be used. Grace said they'd go back to the beginning after that to check everything matched the Amandine sweet and romantic vibe.

Occasionally, Regina became overwhelmed and uncomfortable, and Grace would minimise the image on the screen, and they would talk about business for a while. They discussed marketing in general, the trends in the lingerie industry, and Amandine's history and style.

Once aware that Regina really had no clue when it came to the details of lingerie, Grace started to explain different garments, talking about the differences in cuts, the names, the styles, and more. In return, Regina spoke about her own experience and talked about general best practices for advertising, copywriting, and consumer research.

Time flew by, and it was a surprise to Regina when she noticed it was now dark outside. She glanced at the clock on the screen. "I'm so sorry, it's a quarter to five. I had no idea."

"It's fine," Grace said. "I'm having a great time. I really think that marketing would be a great career move for me if I can find a way to break into the industry. How did you get started?"

Regina chuckled. "Completely by accident. I was working as a receptionist when the owner of the company asked me to put up some posters around the office. They looked terrible, so I redesigned them. Later, he had an ad to go in the local paper, and I redesigned that as well."

Grace sniggered. "Did he mind?"

"He thought I was a pretentious know-it-all, but he let me do what I wanted. And when that ad was the best performing yet, he started to ask me to do more and more. Eventually, I realised I enjoyed it far more than reception work, and I looked for a junior role. I never looked back." Regina leaned back in her chair. "How did you get into modelling?"

"Also by accident," Grace explained. "I was in university and they needed some students for a promo video. I didn't want to do it, but when I realised they'd pay me twenty pounds, I thought why not?"

"Twenty? You were underpaid," Regina said.

Grace laughed. "Absolutely, but I was broke and also really wanted to go to the cinema. Anyway, a while after, I got a message from someone at the production company who told me they had a call from a modelling agency asking if I was available for another ad. I thought it was a con, but she told me they were a legit firm. I called them up and had a chat with the casting director and was called in for a couple of ads for a car firm. I was the woman on the street who turns and looks impressed when a man drives by."

"An essential role," Regina teased.

"Oh, of course! Still, it was a hundred pounds for an afternoon of work. I thought that was great until I met an agent who told me I was undervaluing myself. I signed on with her, and then I moved from ads to modelling. I dropped out of university because I loved it and could see a career in it. And I was struggling with my studies, anyway."

"You were studying psychology?"

"Yes. My professor told me I was making a mistake, but he was a bit of a nightmare, so several people had already dropped out of the course. It was actually him telling me not to do it, and that I'd regret it, that made me decide to go."

"Sounds like you made the right decision."

"I did. I know some people would disagree, but I'm happy."

"Forgive my ignorance, but what sorts of jobs have you done?" Regina asked, keen to learn as much as she could about the fascinating creature she found it so easy to spend time with.

Grace eagerly talked of her career to date, talking about the highs and lows equally. While it was clear that Grace wasn't a superstar model walking the catwalks of famous European cities, she was a successful model who was constantly in demand for a wide range of companies. Grace seemed to have done it all.

Regina happily sat back in her chair and sipped on her now cold tea while she listened to Grace talk. She couldn't remember the last time she found someone so fascinating, nor the last time she found it so easy to talk to someone.

❖

"And it was then I realised that modelling shoes just wasn't for me," Grace said. She laughed at the memory of her slightly wider than average feet being crammed into slim heels.

"That must have been painful," Regina said.

"Not really, I wasn't exactly walking around in them. Just sitting on a table and waving my legs about."

Grace would have enjoyed the slight and adorable blush on Regina's cheeks if at that very moment her stomach hadn't loudly rumbled. She wrapped her hands around her tummy.

"I'm sorry! My stomach gets a bit angry these days. I'm on a new diet on shoot days, and my over-thirty body doesn't like it much. But it's also keen to hold on to any scrap of fat that it can, so it can blame itself."

Regina smiled. "Another reason to go into marketing. Your stomach will thank you." She patted her relatively flat stomach.

"Lots of corporate dinners, and fatty pastries during brainstorming sessions."

Grace chuckled. "Sounds great. Although you might be fibbing, because you look pretty in shape."

Her eyes quickly took in Regina's body. Grace spent her days surrounded by traditionally beautiful women with perfect bodies, but there was something about an average everyday woman that she found irresistible. She'd seen enough gloss and lies in her career. She preferred reality.

"Just for my health," Regina explained. "It's not because someone, or society, has told me to be a certain weight. I'm impressed that you can live with that."

"Mm. I should say that underwear models are at least allowed to have curves and a tiny bit of muscle—some models have it much worse." Grace remembered the start of her career and the quick realisation that the so-called pinnacle of a career in modelling came with unrealistic expectations on her body. She'd picked her jobs carefully, dodging routes into roles that she knew would lead to unhealthy choices.

She loved her job, but she also loved food. And spending every single day in the gym trying to achieve a body that she was genetically unable to maintain wasn't her idea of fun. Of course, she dabbled in the occasional well-researched diet, and she'd grown to enjoy the gym. But both activities were for her own benefit and chosen by her, not dictated by her career.

Her stomach rumbled again, reminding her that it was definitely time to eat. But she didn't want to leave. She didn't know if she would get another opportunity to spend quality private time with Regina. Something about the woman had magnetically attracted Grace to her. Her quiet and reserved confidence competed with the adorable flush on her neck at the hint of skin in a way that fascinated Grace. But long before she knew about Regina's affliction, there had been an attraction, one which sadly seemed to be a one-way street as Regina showed no such interest in Grace at all. She was polite, professional, and even friendly, but nothing more.

"I should get going and grab some dinner before it complains more and scares the whole office." Grace stood up. She pulled the chair back to where she had found it in front of Regina's desk.

"I see we have a shoot for the everyday line tomorrow, whatever that is. Are you booked in for that?" Regina asked.

Grace nodded. "I am. Will you be there?"

Regina sighed. "That will depend on Margot's mood, I imagine."

Grace bit her lip. She wanted to express her desire for Regina to be there but knew that would sound strange. It was too soon. They'd only known each other for a few hours. She didn't want to make Regina feel uncomfortable. She swallowed down her thoughts and simply nodded again. "We'll see then."

"We will. Thank you for your help today—it's really appreciated."

"Thanks for listening to me and not thinking I'm an empty-headed model." Grace picked up the empty bubble tea container and turned to leave. She knew delaying any longer would make it more awkward than it already felt. "Speak soon."

She heard Regina utter a soft goodnight as she quickly passed Arjun's empty desk and raced through the rest of the office in her desire to make a quick getaway. She shook her head at herself. She wasn't usually one to fall for someone in an instant. Crushes were not really her thing. But Regina had come from nowhere and completely captivated her. Worse still, Regina seemed to be absolutely ignorant of Grace's interest in her.

"It's because you're hungry," she muttered to herself. "You'll feel better after you've eaten."

CHAPTER EIGHT

Regina arrived bright and early the next morning, ready to prepare herself for another day and another photo shoot. Margot had emailed her the previous evening to advise her that she'd be managing the shoot that day for the everyday line. She'd also added a sarcastic comment about hoping everything was going well, which Regina knew for certain was the opposite of what she was hoping.

She wasn't going to let Margot get under her skin. Not when the stakes were so high. She needed to prove to Amandine that she could do the job. And, following an evening of scouring the company intranet and looking at the organisation charts, she'd come to the conclusion that Margot didn't hold all the cards. There was a CEO, an operations director, and a head of consumer, all of whom Margot had to report to.

Margot wasn't a fool—she wasn't about to obviously sabotage Regina. Especially when she had vouched for her. No, her plan was clearly to toy with Regina and make her as uncomfortable as possible in the hope that she left, or that the quality of her work was so bad that Margot was left with no choice but to step in and be seen as the saviour. Or, a more disturbing thought, it was Margot's way of trying to get Regina back under her control.

Regina was determined to not let Margot win, and to prove to Amandine that she was able to do the job. Or at least do the job for a year or so until it would be professionally acceptable to move on to another, more suitable role.

As she stepped onto set that morning and caught a glimpse of the models, she began to wonder if she'd finish the week, never mind a year.

The everyday line was more relaxed in style and resembled more day-to-day underwear. It was still fancier than Regina's normal underwear and more along the lines of something she would consider wearing if planning to seduce her lover. Her memory flashed back to her relationship with Margot, who had always taken the lead in any seduction. Now she thought of it, Regina realised that she had never taken the lead with any of her previous lovers. She shook the thought away. Now was not the time to fall down that particular rabbit hole.

Arjun crossed the room to greet her.

"Good morning, can I get you something? Tea?"

Regina smiled at his eagerness to please. "Good morning. No, thank you. I picked up my usual order and drank it on the way in. What you could do is see if there are updated sales projections for all the ranges. I was reading through documents yesterday, and I think Margot may have accidentally sent me out of date figures as they don't include the high street deals made two months ago."

Arjun nodded and grabbed his phone from his pocket. "Sure. Let me check that with business operations and get right back to you."

Thomas approached, camera in hand. "Morning. We're ready to get started if you are."

Regina tried to smile as she offered him a small nod. She took her seat beside him. A tactic she had used the previous day was to position herself behind one of the large screens under the guise of looking at the images there instead of watching what was happening on set. It gave her some cover, but she still wondered how long she'd be able to get away with it.

Thomas got the shoot underway, going through the shoot list and directing the models. Regina had read that it was usual for the shoot manager to direct, which she assumed was herself, but that photographers often wished to do it themselves. Thankfully, Thomas had never given her much option and had immediately taken full control. If he hadn't, she probably would have fainted on day one.

She busied herself on her phone and with her shoot list, pretending to be fully engaged in the shoot but actually trying to do anything but look at the models and photographs flashing up on the screen in front of her. Now and then she saw a flash of something and felt a surge in her chest, but she maintained her breathing exercises and waited for her body to return to normal.

After what seemed like an eternity, but was probably less than an hour, Thomas called for a break. He rushed off to the green room. Regina had noticed the day before that he was obsessed with the pastries the catering company provided.

"Morning."

Regina looked up and swallowed. Grace was standing beside her, meaning Regina's eyeline grazed an expanse of naked skin that she was not at all prepared for. Her eyes snapped down to the paperwork on her lap.

"H-hello. How are you?"

"Would you like me to put a robe on?" Grace asked, her voice soft enough that only Regina could hear.

"Nope. No, it's—um…fine. You have to get back to work soon. It's okay. I'm okay." Regina wished she could do something to stop her mouth from spewing out nonsense, but it seemed to have a mind of its own.

"Are you sure? You nearly strained your optic nerve looking away so fast," Grace said lightly, clearly testing the water as to whether or not the joke would be appreciated.

It was. Regina smiled and very carefully looked up, being mindful to make eye contact with Grace and try to ignore everything else. Her heart slammed against her ribs, and she knew her cheeks were blotchy and red, but she was determined to manage.

"Good morning." Grace smiled and repeated her earlier greeting. "How are you today?"

"I'm well, thank you. And you?"

"I'm good. I bought that book you mentioned, the one on writing compelling marketing copy."

"Oh, good. I have a few others I can recommend. Actually,

some of them are old-fashioned paperbacks, so you can borrow them if you like."

"That would be amazing, thank you." Grace looked hesitant for a moment.

"What is it?" Regina asked, suddenly feeling that she would do anything to bring the smile back to Grace's face.

"I…wanted to ask something, but it's really none of my business."

"Go on," Regina pressed.

"You said you were pushed into this job. I didn't want to pry at the time, but I can't help wondering what you meant. You're clearly suffering being here."

Regina hesitated. It would be good to unburden herself and tell someone. And Grace was extremely easy to speak to.

"What I'm about to tell you has to stay between us," Regina said.

"Of course."

Regina kept her gaze fixed to Grace's, never letting it dip down to snowy underwear against what looked to be perfectly soft skin. "Margot and I dated for a while. We were a terrible match, and I ended things a while ago. I thought she was over it, and we'd never see each other again. Someone dropped out of this role at the same time I posted a public message on LinkedIn about being made redundant."

Regina looked around the room to check no one was able to overhear them. "She arranged for me to get this role. Clearly, she knows of my issue. She's toying with me, trying to make me as uncomfortable as possible."

"That's terrible. Can't you leave?"

"I need the money. I pay for my aunt's care home fees."

"A loan?"

Regina let out a small sigh. "Not without a job, and I can't lie on any application form if I know I'm leaving. Besides, she's issued press releases to marketing journals about me taking this role. If I leave now, it will look very odd. It could really impact my ability to get another job."

Grace looked horrified. "She's trapped you here to mess with you?"

"Essentially, yes."

Horror gave way to anger and Grace folded her arms and shook her head. "Well, that shows you made the right decision in dumping her. Let her do her worst. You'll nail this job, I know you will."

Regina wasn't so sure. After yesterday and the morning so far, she felt nervy, like a coiled spring pulled taut and about to ping back at any moment. A situation that was becoming more acute with Grace's proximity.

Thomas exited the green room and stood in the doorway, a pastry in each hand, as he called out, "By the way, we're done with the group shots for today. Close-ups for the rest of the day."

He walked back into the green room at the same moment that all the models sighed with relief. One of them retrieved a pair of glasses from her bag and put them on. Another removed a hair scrunchy and shook out her long locks.

"Oh, thank goodness," Grace said. She reached up into her hair. "This bun is so tight."

As Regina turned back to Grace, she had started expertly plucking hairpins out of her hair until the updo came undone. Within moments, her hair cascaded over bare shoulders.

In the blink of an eye, Regina felt dizzy. In her haste to look away from the silky locks, she looked at Grace's body instead. All sense of control left her as her gaze slowly took in impossibly soft-looking skin with curves in all the right places.

"I got those updated sales projections," Arjun said, walking over to Regina and jolting her from her stupor.

She jumped up from the chair, eager for an excuse to leave. "Perfect. Email them to me and take over here, please."

"Me?" Arjun looked surprised.

"Yes." She handed Arjun the paperwork. "Keep Thomas on track, soft, relaxed, and natural. And follow the schedule we agreed on yesterday. There shouldn't be any issues."

"All right," Arjun said, running a hand over his neatly groomed beard. "Will you be back soon?"

"This afternoon," she said. It was vague enough to give her time to settle. "When you're finished up here, tell Thomas to send me the files again, and I'll review them before the end of the day."

Arjun sat in her seat and looked at the schedule. "Okay. Sounds good."

She knew she was lucky that Arjun was so confident and professional—other assistants might have folded under the pressure. She ventured a look at Grace, who was frowning with obvious confusion and some concern.

"Thank you for your help, Grace. I'll catch up with you later." She turned to make her escape.

CHAPTER NINE

It was after lunch when Regina returned to the office. She'd walked in the brisk September air until she felt cold to the bone. Then she'd had lunch, which ended up being ice cream and a glass of wine at the bar of a hotel.

Arjun was back at his desk when she returned. He eyed her with a suspicious look. She couldn't blame him. It was more than unusual for your boss, who had been in position for less than two days, to vanish in the middle of an important photo shoot. While Arjun seemed capable of taking over, it was certainly not a job he should have been doing.

"Everything okay?" he asked, attempting to sound casual.

"I'm fine." She tried to smile reassuringly. "I had an important errand to run. Anything to report from the shoot?"

He shook his head. "No, everything went well. Thomas will send the pack when it's finished uploading."

"Wonderful. Could you get me Grace Holland's phone number?"

"Sure." He tapped a search query on his laptop and a moment later jotted down some digits on a sticky note. He handed it to her, again looking like he was trying to size her up and determine what was going on.

She realised there would need to be a bit of work to get Arjun back onside and convince him that she wasn't some flake who vanished in the middle of the day. But first, she needed to apologise to Grace. She entered her office and closed the door. At her desk, she picked up the phone and dialled with slightly shaking hands.

"Grace speaking."

"Hi, Grace. It's Regina."

"Oh hi!" Grace sounded happy to hear from her, which Regina found to be a relief.

"Yes, hi, yes. Um. I hope this isn't a bad time. I just wanted to call and apologise for my behaviour earlier."

"You did leave a bit suddenly—I wondered if you were okay. I'm sorry. I'm so used to walking around in whatever the shoot needs, I don't think to put a robe on unless I'm cold. I should have thought."

"It wasn't your fault. You offered. I just didn't know my limits. I suppose everyone thought I'd lost my mind?"

"I don't think anyone really noticed much. You know what Thomas is like—he just got on with it."

"Good, good. Arjun is watching me like I'm a ticking bomb."

"I think he was worried when you left. I was too," Grace said. "Where did you rush off to?"

"St. James's Park. I go there for long walks every weekend, but also to gather my thoughts when work gets hectic. Or something… happens." Regina sat back in her chair and closed her eyes. "Then I went to a hotel and drowned my embarrassment in a glass of wine and a bowl of ice cream at the bar."

"Ice cream always helps," Grace said softly.

Regina realised she didn't feel confident that Grace had fully heard and accepted her apology. Being on the phone, rather than face to face, made it difficult to read nuance. Regina desperately hoped she hadn't ruined the burgeoning friendship she had with Grace.

"I know this is cheeky, especially following my erratic behaviour this morning, but I'd love to see you face to face to apologise properly."

"I don't think you need to apologise. In fact, I was planning to pop by your office and check over today's shoot with you. If you still want my help?" Grace asked hesitantly.

"Definitely. I value your opinion more than I can say. It would be a great help to have your expert advice again."

Grace sighed with relief. "I'm so glad to hear that. What time should I come by?"

"I have a couple of things to catch up on." Regina glanced at her inbox and calendar. "Is four okay?"

"If we can make it four thirty, I can pop to the gym and go for a swim."

Regina shoved the image of Grace in swimwear out of her mind. "Yes. Sure, four thirty sounds great."

"Perfect! See you then."

❖

At half past four on the dot, there was a knock on Regina's office door. She called for Grace to come in and was relieved to see her warm, genuine smile. She'd spent most of the afternoon worrying that she had ruined things, despite the cordial phone call earlier that afternoon.

Regina launched right in. "I must apologise again for this morning. Not just for running off like that but for, well, what must have looked like open-mouthed gawking. I'm sorry, I'm not like that. I promise."

There was a little smile at Grace's mouth. But it didn't look mocking. It was more…pleased? Coy? Regina couldn't quite place it.

"As I said on the phone, I don't think you need to apologise. I'm sorry I made you uncomfortable but…" Grace paused, the smile still lingering on her lips.

"But?"

Grace closed the door behind her and walked right up to Regina's desk, as close as she could get with the desk separating them. "I kind of like that you looked. That you managed it, I mean. I know that wasn't easy for you."

Regina swallowed. "You didn't mind?"

"No. First of all, people stare at me in underwear constantly. It's my job," Grace said. "Secondly, unlike you, I'm very comfortable with nudity and people's bodies. Humans are just very evolved animals after all. Under our clothes, everyone has meat, skin, and some fur. No big deal. To me, anyway."

Regina had a few things she wanted to say to that. She wanted to highlight that no matter the similarities, there were also some enormous differences from person to person. And that not everyone was as casual about showing off their body as Grace. But she decided she'd been given a second chance and realised it was best to leave it at that.

"I'm glad you're comfortable in your skin," Regina said.

"I am. Especially around you. I know you would never stare at me in a way that made me uncomfortable."

Regina almost frowned. She was sure that was exactly what she had done, leered at Grace in an unacceptable way. But apparently Grace hadn't seen it that way. She wondered if she'd blown the situation out of proportion. In the end, it was irrelevant now, and she had a chance to move on, one she was eager to take up.

"I see. Well, I'm glad we cleared that up."

"Absolutely, water under the bridge," Grace confirmed. "Have today's photos arrived?"

Regina nodded to her laptop. "They have."

Grace clapped her hands together excitedly. "Great." She took the chair and sat it by Regina's.

Grace pulled the laptop close and took control, as she had done the day before. Regina had printed out a couple of updated copies of the shoot schedule for them to make notes and handed Grace a copy.

"I think it went really well today," Grace said. "Thomas pretty much stayed on brief, which isn't always the case."

She started flipping through photos, and Regina felt her pulse spike. They'd barely begun, and she was already feeling the stress of the situation. Thankfully, Grace seemed to notice and blitzed through to the close-up images. They'd figured out that Regina could look at some of the close-ups without too much problem, when it was hard to get the context of what she was looking at.

Of course, that only lasted a while, and soon they were into the standard shots that caused Regina's eyelids to slam shut in self-defence. When that happened, Grace would sit back and encourage Regina to talk about something else.

At first it was previous marketing campaigns, then overall best practices, then career advice. But soon they were running out of generic topics of conversation, and Grace ventured into more personal themes. For some reason, the topic of pets came up, and before long they were both giggling at each other's childhood stories.

"I can't imagine you with a hamster," Grace said.

Regina laughed. "Why not?"

"I don't know, you're just...not like I picture a hamster owner." Grace collapsed into laughter at her own description.

"Well, I was nine at the time," Regina said. "I've changed a little since then. But I think I was a great hamster owner to little Hammy."

"Hammy?" Grace giggled.

"Well, Hamish McAlister was his official name."

Grace's eyes widened. "Why on earth did you name him that?"

"Because the shop owner was Scottish." Regina chuckled. "It made sense at the time."

"I had a cat when I was about that age. I called it Kitty. I clearly didn't have your imagination. Maybe my marketing career is doomed."

"Definitely," Regina agreed. "Interesting pet names are an absolute essential. Might as well give up now if Kitty is the best you have."

Grace gave her arm a light slap as she threw her head back with laughter. Regina couldn't help but beam with pride at making Grace laugh so hard. It really was the most magical sound.

They got back to work and managed to get through all the photos without Regina needing too many more breaks, something she was quite proud of herself for, even if she knew it was mainly because Grace was a delightfully distracting presence.

A notification flashed up on Regina's laptop, and she caught sight of the time. "Oh my, it's five to six. I'm so sorry I've kept you here so long."

"You haven't kept me from anything. I knew what time it was. My stomach started low-key growling a while ago, telling me it was close to dinner time."

Dinner. Regina mindlessly picked up her phone and started slowly turning it over and over in her hand. Could she ask? *Should she ask?*

Her role at Amandine meant she was in a position of power over Grace. She didn't want to abuse that power. Or give Grace the impression that she was playing some long game in order to try to get a date with her. Especially when Regina thought it must be pretty obvious that she found Grace extremely attractive.

Grace leaned in closer. "What are you thinking?"

Regina greedily inhaled the fresh cottony smell which she now associated with Grace. She tossed the question over in her mind one more time before finally saying, "I was thinking that we're both hungry and it's late." She forced herself to say the next words. "Perhaps we should call it a night?"

Grace squinted into the autumnal dark outside the window. "I was planning on getting takeaway tonight. So, if I'm doing that, I might as well eat it here. With you. Unless you have plans?"

"No," Regina said, far too fast. She would do anything for just another moment in Grace's company. "Although, if we do order up some food, I insist you let me charge it to the corporate account."

Amandine had a generous expenses policy—she might as well make use of it.

"I'm not going to argue with that," Grace said, leaning back in her chair and stretching. "I've seen how much Amandine stuff sells for. I was going to buy a bustier that I had modelled and liked. I nearly choked on my own tongue when I saw the price."

Regina shooed off the animal part of her brain that wanted to focus on *bustier* and *tongue* in relation to Grace and just said, "Exactly. They can afford to buy us some dinner."

"But only if we don't talk about work the entire time," Grace added. "I can't eat dinner and talk shop. I need to hear about any other pets and what you might have called them."

Regina smiled. "I'll see what I can do."

"Good, we're off the clock, after all."

Being off the clock wasn't something that had existed much in Regina's life. She loved her work and didn't take much time off. Even when she wasn't working, her mind was close to the subject. However, she wanted to hear more about the cat named Kitty and to hear Grace laugh again.

❖

Grace had nearly sighed a breath of relief when her gamble had paid off. When she'd eaten dinner alone the night before, she wished that she'd been a little braver and asked Regina to eat with her. She'd not been ready to say goodnight and knew that if she got another chance to spend time with Regina, the same thing would happen.

And so she'd decided to be brave and ask Regina to eat with her if she got a chance. She'd reminded herself that the worst that could happen was that she'd say no, which she tried to convince herself wasn't all that bad, but in actual fact would have been fairly soul-destroying.

Thankfully, Regina had said yes and had ordered dinner from a Thai-Malay-British fusion restaurant that she had apparently frequented for years. It came as no surprise to Grace that Regina had a regular order at a restaurant she knew well. She seemed to be someone who found comfort in familiar settings. In the short time they had known each other, it had become very clear that Regina was a creature of habit.

Eager to adapt to the situation, Grace let Regina order for her, and soon two portions of chicken thigh green curry arrived. As they ate, Grace steered the conversation away from work and instead towards television shows and books they'd both read.

It was easy to talk to Regina, a little too easy. Grace found herself laughing and also watching the clock as she noticed the minutes unfairly slipping away at a greater speed than she wished.

It was perfect but for one small thing.

"I've never had lemongrass sparkling water before," Grace said, looking curiously at the bottle it came in.

"It's one of my staples. Like it?"

"Hell no," Grace said, her lips curling into a smile. The taste was unique and something she wasn't likely to ever become accustomed to. But she loved trying new things, and so there was a silver lining, even if it wasn't the drink itself.

Regina couldn't help but smile. "And yet you've nearly finished it."

"Well, it wasn't undrinkable."

"Can I get you something else?" Regina offered. "I found the kitchen this morning. I could—"

"No, no. I'm fine. I can have a drink I don't particularly like now and then. It doesn't matter." Graced smiled. "But next time I'm sticking with my usual Coke Zero."

She hoped there would be a next time. And hoped even more that saying it out loud made it more likely to happen. She still couldn't get a read on Regina's thoughts. She was irritatingly polite and gave no indication whether she was simply being nice by dining with Grace or if she actually enjoyed it.

With the meal finished and conversation drying up, Grace knew it was time to go. On another day she might have taken Regina up on her offer of a hot drink and nursed a mug of tea long after it had gone cold to delay her departure. Sadly, she had things to do, and time was running out.

"I suppose I should get going," Grace said, standing up and clearing things away. "I have lots of laundry to do and an early train to Edinburgh for a shoot tomorrow."

"Will I…" Regina coughed and sipped some sparkling water. "I mean, are you booked for any photo shoots at Amandine in the upcoming weeks?" She stood and helped to clean up the debris from the takeaway.

"Only one that I know of at the moment. Amandine are

famously last minute in making decisions. For once I've gotten an eveningwear gig here. With my body type and looks, it's rare that I get calls for anything but underwear at Amandine. Maybe someone called in sick or something. Anyway, that's on Friday. I might be back to your shoot on Monday, but it's not confirmed yet."

While Grace had been thrilled with the eveningwear gig, she'd now much rather be on the underwear shoots with Regina. It was only Tuesday, and the next time she might even glimpse Regina would be the following week, something that seemed somehow unfair.

There was something tantalising about being in Regina's presence, not least the fact that Grace couldn't figure out what was going on in Regina's mind. She'd casually mentioned that she was single, so Grace felt it safe to push the boundary a little and flirt to see what sort of reaction she got.

She casually approached Regina and pretended to pluck a couple of strands of hair from the lapel of Regina's suit jacket.

"Oh. Thank you," Regina said, glancing down at her lapel. "My aunt says I shed like a cat in spring."

Grace chuckled. She was still none the wiser on whether Regina might be interested in her. Damn the woman for being so mysterious.

"Can I be cheeky and text you if I have any questions about that book I bought? I plan to read it on the train, but I'm already sure it's going to go way over my head," Grace said.

"Of course you can."

Happy for an excuse to get Regina's mobile number, she got out her phone and tapped in the details that Regina reeled off.

"Got it. Thanks," Grace said, tucking the phone into her jacket pocket.

"You're welcome. Text at any time."

Grace wanted to groan. She sounded eager. But did she mean it? The words said yes but the indifferent expression said no.

Throwing caution to the wind, Grace brushed her flat palm over Regina's jacket lapel again. This time she moved slower, savouring the feel.

"Another loose hair," she lied. She kept her gaze on Regina's jacket, worried that making eye contact would give her away.

Regina thanked her again. Grace stepped away. She wondered if she'd overstepped, showing her hand and pushing Regina away at the same time.

"I better get going," she said, grabbing her things and heading to the door without looking back at Regina. "'Night."

As she walked out of Amandine, she shook her head and sighed. Regina was such a closed book; Grace had no idea if she was even mildly interested in her. If only Regina would give her some indication either way, then Grace would know whether to continue flirting or give up.

She smiled to herself. She wouldn't give up easily. Flirting with Regina was fun. It had been a while since Grace had felt genuinely interested in someone. The attraction and the jeopardy were a thrill. She supposed she'd just have to see what their next encounter would bring.

CHAPTER TEN

On Regina's third day at Amandine, she had the opportunity to meet some of the executive team through a number of meetings she was invited to. It was a relief to see that Amandine wasn't all gorgeous women in the latest fashions. In fact, right now she was speaking to a man in his sixties who was wearing a suit that was too big for him and scuffed around the edges.

He was something in the operations team—Regina didn't quite catch the unnecessarily long title but had caught that his name was Ben. The meeting was an introduction and catch up, where Ben was to explain all of the details of his role and how he'd be working with Regina. But so far, he seemed far more interested in learning about Regina.

Regina had been around office politics long enough to know that you never knew who was chummy with who, and so she picked her words carefully. She wanted it to be known that Margot had thrown her into the deep end with the photo shoots, but not to sound as if she was complaining about it. Two could play Margot's game. It also helped that Margot was famously lacking awareness of how others saw her. Her confidence was so high that she just naturally assumed everyone liked her, not always the reality due to Margot being…well, Margot.

When Regina had finished casually speaking of her first two roller coaster days, Ben looked a little shocked.

"Was Margot there?" he asked.

"No, she left me to it. She gave me the impression it was usual to need employees to hit the ground running. Felt a little sink or swim to me, but luckily I have a lot of experience with photo shoots and managed to get through the brand guidelines quickly enough. We have some fantastic shots we can use."

A crease in Ben's brow let Regina know that her comments had hit just right. She wasn't going to be seen as complaining, or dropping Margot in it, just chatting about her first couple of days on the job. If Margot could sabotage, then so could she.

Not that it was really sabotage to be alerting colleagues to the fact that Margot was making dicey business decisions, to say the least. And it was nothing in comparison to what Margot was really putting her through.

Later that afternoon, Regina was back in her office, enjoying a cup of tea. It had been a hectic day of meetings, but at least now Regina felt as though she knew a bit more about Amandine and its leadership team. She no longer felt trapped beneath Margot's seniority and had started to build working relationships with other people.

The sound of heels clicking like daggers in ice told her that Margot was on her way.

She took a long sip of sugary tea to reinforce herself against what was on the way.

Margot burst into the office without knocking and slammed the door behind her. She'd always been dramatic, but Regina had really thought she'd tone it down in an office environment.

"Good afternoon, Margot." Regina leaned back in her chair and cupped her tea mug. "And how are you today?"

"How am I? How am I?" Margot seethed. "I'm considering snapping your neck, that's how I am."

Regina wasn't put off by the rage flowing from Margot. She'd been used to it once before and she was becoming used to it again.

She was all smoke and no fire. And if she was this upset, then Regina's sabotage had clearly hit the right notes.

"In a professional environment, you might want to stick with a hello and either *I'm well* or *Actually, I have something on my mind.* Just a suggestion."

Margot advanced like a thunderstorm, slamming her hands on Regina's desk.

"I was contacted by HR to talk about my management style and my decision to not oversee your work. Apparently, they'd had complaints. Complaints, Regina, with an *s*."

"How extraordinary," Regina said. "I certainly didn't say a thing."

"Well, someone did. So I had to tell them that Regina Avery doesn't need overseeing. But they suggested that a little more oversight was required. I cannot believe you actually ran off to"— flushed with rage, Margot halted, clearly searching for words—"tell the teacher that I bullied you."

"I didn't," Regina said, jaw tight. "If I was doing that, I'd mention that you hired someone with something very close to a phobia with the plan to submit them to their trigger issue in order to get revenge on them for dumping you. While also publicly announcing their new role, with the view to holding them in that role for as long as possible for your own pleasure."

"Well, whatever you did, it's backfired for you because I have been asked to shadow you closer. Much closer."

Regina swallowed. Backfire was an understatement. She couldn't believe she'd been so stupid. Of course the leadership would give Margot the opportunity to fix her mistake. Modern business was about giving people chances, not throwing them under the bus or replacing them the moment a small hitch happened.

"Well, we don't have to do that," Regina said. "We could say that was happening but ultimately carry on as we are. Ignoring each other."

Margot stood and frowned. "Why would I have brought you here if I wanted to ignore you?"

"To make my life hell?" Regina suggested.

"For a while, yes. I wanted to let you suffer during a couple of the shoots, but after that I had always intended for us to work closer together."

Regina held her breath. She didn't know if this was a bluff to save Margot's precious feelings. It wasn't unusual for Margot to pretend that her plan all along had been something different, just to save face. Admitting fault was something she'd never knowingly done.

The alternative was that Margot was seriously intending to attempt to get Regina back, to toy with her a little and then somehow get her caught back up in the web, something Regina would never let happen. But if she rejected Margot again, who knew what her next steps would be.

The phone on Regina's desk rang.

Margot looked at the display and picked up the call.

"Hello?…Oh, hello, Lawrence…No, it's Margot. I was just with Regina, going through our coaching plan."

Regina watched as Margot casually lied to the operations director. Margot was looking directly at Regina as she spoke, a wicked smile on her face.

"Absolutely, we'll come up to the boardroom now." Margot hung up the call. "Time to go and show everyone our new partnership. Come, Regina."

Regina stood and followed her. It seemed that things had just gotten far more complicated for her.

Chapter Eleven

Regina's Thursday morning started terribly with a text message from Margot before she'd even left home. The short message demanded Regina come to Margot's office as soon as she arrived so they could work on the media spend portion of the campaign.

Unfortunately, that was something Regina would need Margot's assistance with. While she'd been responsible for countless millions in ad spend over the course of her life, she needed to know Amandine's budget and existing providers to pull together a successful series of campaigns.

She sent back a quick reply when another text came in, this time from Grace. If the first text had infuriated her, the second had instantly calmed her irritable mood. Grace was asking if she could pop by Regina's office the following day in the afternoon to discuss a marketing qualification she'd seen. Grace had also added an offer to bring Regina a cup of tea—black, milk, two sugars—as part of the deal.

Regina paused and wondered if she was really that predictable. Grace had known her less than a week and already knew her tea order. She wondered if she should request something else so she didn't appear so boring. In the end, she relented. She *was* that boring. As much as she'd like to think she could jump out of her tried and tested daily grind, she didn't want to.

And so, she texted back that she'd love to see Grace and added that she'd also like the offered cup of tea.

The walk to the office was pleasant enough, save for the fact that she found herself grinding her teeth at Margot's summoning her first thing. She had hoped that she'd be able to spend a little time on her own before Margot decided to begin their new shadowing agreement.

There was also the conversation from the previous day which had left Regina a little concerned. Margot was very good at rewriting history, Regina had seen it many times when they were together. One moment they were arguing, and the next Margot would be grinning and claiming it was all a joke and there was nothing to argue about. All of which made it difficult to know what Margot was really thinking and what she was planning to do next.

❖

Regina hadn't been in Margot's office before, deliberately trying to avoid the dragon's den, so she was surprised to note that it wasn't the bright white colours of Amandine. Instead, there were blacks and greys, not dark but certainly not matching the rest of the offices around her.

It reminded Regina of the times when Margot had encouraged Regina to stop buying black suits and try charcoal grey instead. Regina hadn't liked being told what to wear but also had to admit that she preferred the shade of grey.

Margot was smiling, which made Regina want to turn around and leave again.

"Regina! Good morning, come in, take a seat over there." She gestured to a table and two chairs set up by the window.

"Morning," Regina returned warily. She took a seat and placed her notebook and MacBook down on the table.

"I'm sure that between us we'll get this all mapped out in no time," Margot said. She stood and gathered some papers. "And then I'd like us to brainstorm phase two of the launch for the European market. We'll no doubt be able to deliver some fantastic ideas to the board."

"Sure." Regina didn't know why Margot was feeling so positive and wanted to tread very carefully.

Margot's smile vanished in the blink of an eye. "No need to sound so sceptical. We're going to achieve a lot together. Unless your negative attitude is going to stand in the way?"

"No negative attitude." Regina held up her hands in a placating gesture.

"Good, I'm glad." Margot placed her papers on the table and sat down. "Let's get started with the budget."

❖

They worked until the early afternoon without a break. Regina felt every single moment tick by. Throughout, Margot blew hot and cold. One moment she was charming and full of compliments, and the next she'd flip to an icy glare and a cutting comment.

Regina tried to not react to either. Her plan was to get through the day and hope that the next day would bring better. Maybe Margot would bore of Regina given time.

Margot peeled a sticky note from one of Regina's notes and laughed as if she was at a comedy spectacular starring her favourite comedian.

"Oh, Regina, you do make me laugh."

Considering she was clearly laughing *at* rather than *with*, Regina didn't react.

"You have a natural talent for marketing, and your work ethic really does you proud," Margot said. "But you're starting to slack."

Regina raised an eyebrow. She knew Margot was trying to get a reaction from her, and she was determined to not give one. But the idea of even accusing Regina of slacking was perplexing to say the least, especially considering she was using a scribbled note as the basis of the accusation.

"I remember when we worked on that condiments campaign, all those months ago. You became practically the world leading expert on every flavour of mustard in a couple of days." Her laughter turned to a pout. "And yet you don't know the difference between a balcony bra and a plunge bra. There's no balcony bra in this line, dear."

Regina grimaced at the mistake. She needed to get a handle on the naming conventions used in all the lines. From her perspective, everything was either a bra, knickers, or something akin to a posh nightie. She knew that was simplifying something in such a way that would probably offend many people, but it just wasn't her area of expertise.

She'd stumbled upon a bra type and size that seemed to fit her years before, and she'd bought the exact same one in bulk every year and prayed that the manufacturer would keep producing it.

"A mistake—we've not eaten lunch yet, and this is my fourth day," Regina replied. "Besides, despite my supposed slacking, the photo shoots came out well. You said so yourself."

"I did?"

"Yes," Regina grumbled, tired of these mind games. "Only ten minutes ago."

Margot sniggered. "I know, I know. I'm teasing you. Banter, you know?"

Margot didn't banter. She switched direction like a race car flying haphazardly around hairpin bends. Anything to cover her tracks when she'd made a mistake.

"Well, maybe less banter and more work?" Regina suggested. "Get this finished so we can get back to other tasks? And maybe have some lunch?"

Margot grinned. "There's that work ethic I admire so much. It's actually a very sexy trait, Regina. I think it's what first drew me to you."

Regina stared for what felt like a lifetime before stammering, "S-sexy?"

Margot smiled. "Extremely. I miss that time together. Working together during the days. Being together during the nights."

Regina recoiled. "Margot. Please. Don't mess with me like this."

"What do you mean?"

Regina waited a moment while she considered her words very carefully. She didn't want to send Margot into a flying rage, but also she wanted to be absolutely clear that she had no interest in Margot whatsoever. She decided the best way to approach the conversation was to leave Margot a clear path out of the mess she was getting herself into. An escape route that wouldn't result in embarrassment when Regina rejected her. Again.

"I mean, you obviously don't have any lingering romantic interest in me. You made that very clear."

A devilish smile grew on Margot's lips. "But you can be quite beguiling, Regina. Maybe I was hasty to end things."

Regina blinked. She was seriously starting to wonder if Margot was all right. Her ability to rewrite history was scary.

"I could make you very happy," Margot continued. "We could forget the awfulness of our break-up. If only you would commit to me. Fully."

Regina could almost hear the sound of the iron shackles that Margot presumably had in mind when she spoke of commitment. She knew she had to be very clear but also very careful. She needed Margot to know that she had no interest in her, but also to not upset her so much that she made Regina's life more of a living hell than she'd already planned to do.

"Margot, I…don't think of you like that. You're a…captivating woman, and we had some lovely times together. Nevertheless, you are my manager now. Nothing more."

Margot's smile started to vanish. A look of something approaching desperation took its place. "But we're a perfect match. You can't deny that."

"Margot, just a couple of days ago you were threatening my livelihood for dumping you," Regina reminded her.

"All games, Regina! You knew that. And *I* dumped *you*, remember. You forgot my parents' names. It was the last straw."

Regina felt anger course through her. She wasn't about to accept Margot's rewriting of history anymore. A few minutes in Margot's sphere of madness was enough to remind her just how twisted the woman could be. Suddenly, she didn't care if she was out of a job. The truth would be said.

"No. I broke up with you because you were jealous and possessive. Remember? It made you so furious that you threw away everything I left at your house."

Margot waved the accusation away. "A few of your cheap high street suits and a toothbrush."

"An iPhone, all of my work notes for an important client, my only pair of pyjamas which you insisted I bought and wore, and my new credit card."

"My parents really liked you," Margot continued as if Regina hadn't spoken. "To think of you standing there, gaping like a fish, unable to even remember two simple names."

"I'd met them once! And you never spoke about them. Are you even listening to me? You didn't dump me for not remembering their names—I dumped you."

Margot's expression became pure steel. "We can agree to disagree. And there's nothing that cannot be undone. We could be happy if you wanted. If you were willing to allow yourself to be happy."

Regina vowed there and then that she would return to her job search the very second she escaped Margot's office. There was a possibility that something might come up and she could parachute out of Amandine and into somewhere else. Anywhere else. To hell with how bad it looked to be somewhere for such a short period of time. She couldn't stay and continue to work for this unhinged, controlling narcissist much longer.

"Margot, listen to me very carefully. I don't want us to be back together."

"Oh? Are you seeing someone else?" Margot narrowed her eyes and peered at Regina as if she was an interesting problem.

"No."

"Hmm." Margot continued to look at her for a moment before she shrugged. "We really must get back to work. We will discuss this topic later."

"We will?"

"Yes, I'll put something in your diary," Margot said distractedly while tapping away on her phone.

Considering the very real possibility that Margot was now completely unhinged, Regina remained silent. Telling Margot the truth didn't seem to work. How did you argue with someone who would deny whatever you told them and create their own preferred narrative?

"Those fools," Margot muttered. "How many times do I need to tell people to check with me before putting a meeting in my calendar? Honestly, technology has made everyone so entitled. You wouldn't open someone's paper calendar on their desk and add whatever you wanted, would you? No. But here we are with those fools from accounts wanting to have a meeting with me this afternoon."

Margot's voice rose so high at the end that Regina winced a little. Margot must have read her expression as agreement. She continued her rant. "No explanation. No, just a chat. A chat. But you can guarantee that chat will be about something. And I'll not have had any time to prepare. This is maddening. As if I have nothing better to do." She stood up. "Stay here. I'm going to go down there and speak to them about this. If they like putting unscheduled meetings in my calendar, then they should be delighted when I have one by their desk with no notice."

Regina couldn't imagine anyone being delighted by Margot's sudden and unplanned presence. She wondered how she'd managed to get the job at Amandine before reminding herself that Margot did have a reasonably good guest face when she could be bothered to bring it out. It was how Regina had ended up dating her. If she'd had the slightest clue what Margot was really like, she would have run a mile.

"Take your time," Regina said, looking forward to a few moments alone.

Margot didn't appear to be listening as she stormed out of the office.

Regina sat back in the chair, blowing out a long breath. She had to clear her mind of Margot, not easy when her signature perfume lay heavily in the office like someone had brought a bath full of potpourri into the room.

Unable to work, she pulled out her mobile phone and toyed with the idea of texting Grace. Grace was the absolute opposite to Margot in so many ways, not just in looks and age, but in her mindset and outlook. She laughed when she was with Grace in a way she'd never laughed with Margot. And she'd been honest, even about her darkest secret, within moments of meeting Grace.

There was nothing there, of course. It wouldn't have been right considering their positions, not to mention Grace being far too young and attractive to want anything to do with Regina beyond a friendly face and maybe a mentor.

After much deliberation about what to put in the text, she settled on a simple hello and asked how the shoot was going. The message was read straight away, and three dots indicated that Grace was replying immediately.

Grace said things were going well and asked how Regina's day was going. She hesitated, wondering if she should be honest or tell a little white lie for the sake of polite conversation. In the end, she decided to go for the middle option, not telling Grace everything but mentioning that she was trapped with Margot for the day but was thankfully having a respite as Margot had gone to shout at someone.

A few seconds after the text had been sent, Regina's phone rang. It was Grace. Regina smiled so wide that she felt the muscles in her cheeks ache.

"Hello there," she said.

"Hi, I thought I should offer my sympathies vocally," Grace joked.

"Thank you, thank you. It's a trying time," Regina replied, playing along. "She's already mocked me for not being any good at my job, so it's about what I was expecting, I suppose."

"Why did she say that?" Grace asked, sounding affronted.

"Because I don't know the difference between a balcony bra and a plunge bra."

"I can explain the differences to you," Grace offered. No pity, no mockery, and no game-playing, Grace simply wanted to help, and Regina couldn't help but smile some more.

"That would be wonderful, thank you."

"No problem. I'm looking forward to seeing you tomorrow," Grace said. "I mean, if you still have time to discuss that course I saw?"

"Absolutely," Regina agreed. "You're bringing me tea, remember?"

Grace chuckled. "It's a cheap price to pay. Oh, I better go—we're being called to set again. Good luck with the dragon."

Regina laughed and said goodbye. She placed the phone on the table and looked out of the window. Just a short call with Grace and she was already feeling much calmer than before. Now she just hoped she could escape from Margot's clutches the next afternoon.

Chapter Twelve

Regina yawned long and loud. It wasn't something she'd usually do on a crowded Tube train, but she was exhausted. So exhausted in fact that she had overslept and was in danger of being late for work if she walked to the office as she often did. So she had no option but to jump on the Tube and yawn at all of the other commuters.

Not that anyone noticed her. No one noticed anyone else on the London Underground. It was the most anonymous form of travel Regina knew. Bleary-eyed commuters focused on books or magazines, or simply closed their eyes and listened to music.

Regina hadn't brought anything with her to pass the time, nothing other than the panic from spending most of the evening scouring every online job board she could possibly find to look for a new job and finding nothing at all.

While she'd only been at Amandine for four days, it felt like a lifetime. Which meant Regina was very surprised when she looked online and found that only a tiny handful of new jobs had become available since the last time she looked. For a while, she had refreshed her browser thinking that something was wrong. But then she sadly realised that it was because hardly any time had passed since her last search. The stress Margot was putting her under meant that every day at Amandine felt like several weeks.

Margot. Regina shivered. The woman was clearly unwell. Not that Regina had a chance of convincing anyone of the fact. Margot was careful in concealing her real nature. Regina had seen that up close a couple of times the previous day when someone had dropped by Margot's office and she'd presented as a stable, nice, normal person. Regina felt as though she was trapped in a psychological drama, the only one who really saw the villain for who she was.

She got off the train a couple of stops before the office to visit her favourite chain cafe and order a cup of tea. The caffeine and the walk would be needed to prepare her for the last day of the week at Amandine.

Images of Margot lurking around every corner, desperate to get them back together, had haunted her dreams. In any other company, Regina would consider contacting HR and making a complaint. But she knew for certain that Margot would make that backfire on her spectacularly. She had Regina cornered, and she wouldn't hesitate to use anything to her advantage.

Takeaway tea in hand, she started the short walk to the office. Her mobile rang, and while balancing her takeaway tea, she checked the screen. Concern that it would be Margot quickly gave way to a much stronger concern when she noted the call was coming from Calm Acres.

"Regina speaking," she answered breathlessly. Her pulse was skyrocketing with worry about why Aunt Bess's care home would be calling her at seven thirty in the morning.

"Good morning, poppet," Bess said as if nothing unusual was happening.

"Morning. You scared me. You never ring this early. You're never up this early."

"Did you think they were calling to tell you that I'd shuffled off this mortal coil?" Bess chuckled.

"Actually, yes," Regina admitted.

"No such luck. You'll have to wait a while longer before you inherit my Royal Family memorabilia collection," Bess joked.

"But I love the Charles and Di tea towel," Regina teased.

"I swear his ears were bigger back then," Bess said.

"It was the eighties—everything was bigger. But, really, why are you calling so early?" Regina noticed the traffic light's switch to red and quickly crossed the road, passing between a double-decker bus and the beeping crossing indicator.

"What was that? Hello?"

"I'm just crossing the road," Regina explained.

"Terrible racket. Honestly, I don't know how you cope with mobile phones all the time. All that noise. You can't hear your conversation any more. Whatever happened to just sitting down and speaking to someone over a normal phone, with a cable?"

"You sound a hundred years old," Regina said. "What's next? Electricity being the devil's magic? You love your iPad."

"Only because I can play my Sherlock Holmes game. No, if I'm having a proper phone call, then I want to sit down and give that person my full attention."

Regina bit her tongue. She was well aware of that fact based on the two- to three-hour long phone calls they had once every couple of weeks, conversations that happened despite having already said everything they could possibly say to one another in person at one of Regina's visits to Calm Acres.

"Well, I'm sorry that I can't give you more of my attention, but I need to get to work," Regina said.

"I know, I know. It's half past seven—you're just arriving at the office. You're a creature of habit, just like your father was."

Regina laughed a little nervously. It was true. She was arriving at work the same time as she always did. The only issue was that she'd neglected to mention to Bess that she was now working for a completely different company.

She'd always told Bess everything, but this was a different matter. This was something that she hadn't quite figured out how to broach yet. Bess knew of Regina's sensitivity around nudity, and one mention of what Amandine sold and what Regina was working on would lead to some uncomfortable questions. Before long, Bess would know the whole story about being made redundant, being back near Margot, and being stuck at Amandine.

Bess would know that it was to pay for her care, and the guilt she'd feel would be tremendous. Regina couldn't do that to her. The less she knew, the better.

"Are you there?" Bess shouted.

"Yes, I'm here."

"Why aren't you saying anything?"

Regina smiled. "I don't know. Nothing much to say, I guess. And you rang me, remember?"

"Mainly because you're the only person I know who would be awake at this awful hour."

"Oh, thank you. I feel so special and appreciated," Regina joked.

"You're being facetious. Did you skip breakfast?"

Regina rolled her eyes. There were times that being mothered by her aunt were appreciated and times when it was not. "No."

"What did you have? Something sugary, I bet."

"Yoghurt and fruit."

"Ah, everything a growing forty-five-year-old needs," Bess said.

"I'm forty-four."

"No, you're not," Bess scoffed.

"I really am. Anyway, as much as I'd love to debate my own age with you, I'm nearly at the office. Did you need something? Other than to talk to the only person you know who is awake at this time?" Regina knew when her aunt was beating around the bush. There was a reason for the call, but for some reason, Bess seemed to be nervous in approaching it.

"Well, yes, I wanted to talk to you about something," Bess confessed, her tone suddenly shy.

Regina paused on the pavement a moment, unable to remember the last time she heard her aunt sound so…little.

"Do you remember the Go Fish game?" Bess continued.

"I do."

"Well, we were playing to decide which men we'd be able to approach for a nice dinner or a trip to the cinema, that kind of thing."

"I remember."

"Well, I managed to win Leonard," Bess explained.

"You mean you won the chance to ask Leonard out?" Regina clarified.

"Yes. Well, we've been out twice—"

"Already? That's fast," Regina said.

"You don't hang around at my age, poppet. Especially with a man like Leonard."

"Who even is Leonard?" Regina asked. Bess was encyclopaedic in her tales about everyone who lived in Calm Acres, but she was fairly sure that she'd never heard of a Leonard before.

Bess launched into Leonard's biography with gusto. He was a widower and a newcomer to Calm Acres, having arrived two weeks ago. He'd kept to himself for the first few days before joining the gardening club and becoming quite popular. He could cook and used to be something high up in the NHS, which apparently meant he had a very good pension. He had two children and four grandchildren.

Regina continued walking to the office, very aware that Bess had barely scratched the surface on what she wanted to divulge on her new man.

By the time she'd arrived at the office, Bess's tone was changing to a more subdued one. "Sadly, this has upset Elsie a bit."

"Elsie?" Regina said, wondering what Bess's best friend had to do with this.

"Yes, she was quite taken with Leonard. But he never felt the same. You see, he'd asked me out once before, but I said no because I thought Elsie would be upset. That's why we played Go Fish—I can always beat Elsie at Go Fish because she always forgets what everyone has. So, I thought, if I can sort of…*win* the right to ask him out, Elsie would be okay with it. And she is. Fair's fair. But now I think I'm falling in love with Leonard."

Regina smiled. "Well, that should be a thing to celebrate and be happy about. What does Elise say about all this?"

"That I should grab on to the chance for love and companionship. That there's no point in us all being miserable." Bess sighed. "Even with her blessing, it's still hard."

"I know," Regina said, hoping to reassure her aunt. "But Elsie wants to see you happy. She'll probably find someone, too, soon."

"I hope so. Leonard is already becoming such an important part of my life. I haven't felt this in love since…I don't even know when. Maybe never. I think this lovely man, my lovely Leonard, is the most special person I've ever met."

Regina walked into Amandine HQ and made her way to her office. As happy as she was for Bess, it did add an extra pressure to her. If Regina couldn't keep her job, then not only would Bess lose her home and friends, but now she'd also lose her new love.

"I'm really happy for you," Regina said. "And I look forward to meeting him."

"He's looking forward to meeting you, too. I've told him all about you."

"Not everything, I hope." She entered her office, placed her tea on the desk, and sat down.

"Well, I started with the story about when you were three and showed that cashier in Tesco your bum. It's a classic," Bess joked. At least, Regina hoped it was a joke. "I better let you get to work. Thank you for listening to me. It helped to talk."

"I'm glad. We'll catch up soon."

They exchanged goodbyes, and Regina hung up. She blew out a long breath, filled with mixed emotions.

It was a while later when Arjun arrived and greeted her, shaking her from her thoughts. She pushed away her takeaway cup of tea—half drunk and lukewarm—and buried herself in emails.

Chapter Thirteen

The day turned out to be quite pleasant, especially when Regina heard that Margot was going to be out of the office most of the day with the CEO, visiting a supplier. Strangely enough, Margot didn't complain when a last-minute meeting was put in her calendar by the CEO's executive assistant. As Regina suspected, it was just another way that Margot liked to flex her authority over others.

Still, Regina decided not to give Margot the satisfaction of taking up space in her thoughts and spent a blissful Margot-free day getting work done and preparing as much as she could for the launch of the lingerie lines.

No matter how engrossed she was in her work, the excitement of Grace coming by that afternoon lingered at the back of her mind. It felt strange to be mildly preoccupied by someone's impending arrival. Regina had always been able to dive into work and not come up for air for hours. In the past, she'd worked through meals, office hours, and a fire drill all without noticing.

Now she occasionally found herself glancing at the clock to count down the hours and minutes until Grace's arrival. The knowledge that she was downstairs shooting an eveningwear line was niggling at her brain. She'd tossed aside several excuses to go down and happen to be passing through, just to get a glance of Grace or even exchange a few words.

There was no denying it. She was utterly smitten with Grace. Not because of her looks, although she was without a doubt the most beautiful woman Regina could even imagine, but because of who Grace was as an individual. Kindness, humour, and a surprising amount of insight made spending time with Grace an absolute joy.

Regina had to constantly remind herself that they were work colleagues and nothing more. Possibly friends, she allowed, with a smile. But the chasm between them in age, interests, appearance, and experiences meant that anything else was impossible. Not to mention the fact that Regina's role meant that she was in a position of authority over Grace, even if she wasn't her direct employer.

All of that meant that Regina had to push any feelings aside and act with absolute professionalism. Even though Grace made it so hard by being so casually down to earth.

The object of her thoughts entered the room with two takeaway mugs, one a see-through bubble tea mix that still confused Regina greatly. The other was placed on her desk as Grace said, "One black tea, two sugars, with milk."

"Thank you, that's very kind." Regina couldn't help but stare. Grace wore an off-the-shoulder sweater, black trousers, and white trainers. The white trainers were clearly of interest to Grace as she lifted her foot in the air.

"Aren't these so cute?"

"Adorable," Regina said, not caring at all about the footwear.

"I saw them in Edinburgh yesterday. I was with some of the girls from the shoot, and our train was cancelled—as usual—so we hit the shops. I saw these, and I had to have them."

Regina took another look at the shoes. She wasn't sure what to say. They were shoes. Nothing more, nothing less. The only thing she knew about shoes was to make sure you could wiggle your big toe.

"Nice," she said. "They look…comfortable."

"They are," Grace agreed. "Like gloves. For feet."

"Which is really all shoes are," Regina said. She picked up her drink and took a sip, anything to give her an excuse to stop speaking.

Grace closed the door and sat in the chair opposite Regina. "And now I have to move, like, next week."

"Move?"

"Yeah, move apartment."

Regina frowned. "Why?"

"Well, first, my landlord has been trying to put my rent up for the last six months. But he'd already put it up eight months ago, and I had it put it into my contract that he couldn't do it again for at least another year. But he keeps trying, keeps talking about interest rates, blah blah."

Regina chuckled but also felt impressed that Grace was someone who thought to implement a rent freeze on her landlord following an increase. Most people felt beholden to their landlords, especially in the busy London market, and would never do anything that might upset them.

"But the other reason is that my neighbour is back in town, and he is so noisy, playing the guitar all night and partying. I mean, I don't mind a party, but I also like my sleep."

"Why is he playing the guitar all night?"

"He's a musician, in some band. I was so happy when he went off on his world tour—everything was so peaceful. But he'll be back this week, and between him and the landlord, I told my agent I want to move, and he's being an angel and looking for something for me."

Regina sipped her tea to hide her surprise. Not that she should have been surprised. Of course, as a model who was constantly in work, Grace had an agent who would help her move. As long as Grace was working, the agent was earning commission. Regina thought that she, too, would turn into a moving service in that situation.

"Maybe he'll have mellowed while he's been touring," Regina said.

Grace made a face. "I don't think so. He's pretty much been this way for as long as he's been making music. He loves touring, so he is usually away more than he's home. But it's my landlord—I know he is looking for any reason to squeeze some more money out of us. He's already raised everyone else's rent, and he's tried to increase my service charge because the concierge is now working twenty-four hours. But I never use the concierge."

"Sounds like you should move," Regina agreed.

"Yes. Somewhere nice and quiet, but still accessible. It will be nice to move and redecorate. I'm sorry, I'm going on and on about me. How are you? Is Margot still stalking you?"

Regina shook her head. "Not today, thank goodness. She's out at some meeting. But yesterday was difficult."

"Do you think she'll get bored and leave you alone at some point?"

Regina wanted to say yes, but she suspected not. Although Margot was so unpredictable, it was difficult to know what she'd do next. But she'd made it clear that she wanted Regina back. Regina couldn't imagine that she'd give up that easily, especially considering the elaborate trap she'd set for her.

"Who knows? Let's not talk about her, I'm enjoying my Margot-free day. How was your shoot downstairs? Eveningwear, wasn't it?" Regina knew very well that it was eveningwear. She'd spent some time exploring what the range was as well as looking at all upcoming shoots to know when Grace was next booked into the Amandine offices.

A moment of panic had washed over her when she'd realised that there had to be a time when all the products had been photographed and the sets shut down until the next range was ready. She'd been right to worry. In just four weeks, all the sets were to be closed and not reopened for Amandine for another six months when they were due to launch the winter season.

Not having a reason to see Grace every day had weighed heavily on her until she reminded herself that might just be a good thing, considering how quickly she had fallen for Grace.

"Yes, it was a hard one."

"I'm sorry to hear that," Regina said sincerely. "How so?"

"The photographer is brilliant, but she's very thorough, and a lot of the eveningwear shots are for the big poster campaigns, so there's a lot more physical work. It's not all standing still and maintaining facial expressions—it's more pausing mid-motion. Still, that's the price you pay for perfection, I suppose."

"Perfection. Yes." She realised she was staring and took another sip of tea. "You got plenty of breaks, at least, I hope?"

Grace smiled and Regina realised she was being overprotecting.

She'd noticed quickly that Margot's setting up of the lingerie shoots hadn't followed normal Amandine procedure regarding breaks and notice given ahead of shoots. Two things that Regina had quickly made sure were implemented.

"Yes, plenty of breaks." Grace smiled warmly at her, and Regina started to get lost in her eyes. "But how about you? Good day so far?"

Regina blinked and brought herself back to the present. "Yes. I had a very interesting conversation with my aunt this morning."

"Oh? What about?"

"She's in love. At the ripe old age of eighty-one. A new man at her care home and she's completely besotted."

"Aww, that's so sweet."

"It is. Although I do worry a little."

"How so?"

"We're very alike—we fall for people very quickly and then dive right in without really looking," Regina confessed. "But I might simply be projecting my feelings, considering how badly things went with Margot. Being here has reminded me how awful that relationship was."

"Just because you had a bad experience doesn't mean you won't have a good one. Or that your aunt hasn't found the man of her dreams," Grace said. "Falling in love quickly can sometimes mean that you know exactly what you're looking for, and when you find it, you don't want to let it go."

"I do hope so," Regina said. "She's been lonely for years, and I'm really happy that she's found someone. She sounded so happy on her call this morning. I just can't help but worry a little. Or maybe I'm just jealous that she's got a more active dating life than I do." Realising that she was oversharing, she quickly pivoted. "But I shouldn't be taking up your valuable time with things like this. Especially if you're going to be moving next week, I imagine you have a lot to do."

Grace hesitated a moment. "Are you busy? I mean, I could come back."

"No, no, I'm just aware that *you* might be busy."

"I'm free for the rest of the day," Grace said. "And I was kind of hoping to get your thoughts on this course I saw. If you're still okay to do that?"

"Absolutely."

Grace stood up, walked around Regina's desk, and gestured to her laptop. "May I?"

Regina nodded. Grace stood so close that Regina could smell her perfume and hear the soft sounds of her breathing. She sucked in a breath and held it, worried that Grace would somehow be able to detect the slamming of her heart against her ribcage.

Grace typed a website address into the search bar, and a familiar website popped up. There were many accreditations someone wishing to get into marketing could gain, and Regina had always made it her business to know them all. Whenever she was hiring, she needed to know if someone had worked through a proper course or just bought a qualification from some internet scammer.

"It looks good—I'd learn a lot," Grace said. "The reviews are good, and it's pricey, which makes me think it's good."

Regina smiled. "It is a good course. I actually know someone who took this course a year or so ago. Would you like me to put you in touch with them so you can discuss it?"

"That would be amazing, thank you." Grace stood up straight and placed her hand on Regina's shoulder. She looked down at her with bright, excited eyes and said, "If I have any questions about the course, can I pick your brain? I mean, I know the coursework should train me, but sometimes I'm better speaking through real-life examples."

In that moment, Regina knew she would have said yes to anything Grace asked her.

"Of course," she breathed. "I'd be happy to."

Grace continued to look down at Regina, and time seemed to stand still. Regina knew she had to say something, or her obvious crush would be revealed, but no words came to her.

The moment was broken by her phone ringing. Grace removed her hand and walked back around the desk to give Regina some space.

She looked at the caller ID and noted it was Margot's PA.

"Hello?" Regina answered.

"Hi Regina, it's Lucy. Margot is going to be out on Monday, so she'd like to push the meeting with you to Tuesday. Is that okay?"

"Yes, that's fine," Regina said, resisting the urge to clap her hands together with glee and shriek with excitement.

Details arranged, she hung up the call. "Seems Margot is going to be out on Monday, too." She couldn't keep the joy from her voice.

"Phew, that must be nice to hear," Grace said.

"It is. I might even celebrate."

"Would you like to come out with me and some friends tonight?" Grace offered. "We're heading to a bar, really casual place but great food. There will be around ten of us, not all models, I promise!"

Regina considered it for a moment longer than she ordinarily would have. Going out for drinks sounded like an absolute nightmare. She liked quiet, early evenings and hadn't been out drinking on a Friday night for over a decade. On top of finding it far too overwhelming, she also couldn't hold her drink like she used to. One glass of wine—and it was always wine—and she found herself starting to get giggly or sleepy. Neither of which would be appropriate with a group of Grace's friends.

It would be embarrassing to admit that her idea of celebrating was picking a unique flavour of ice cream and watching a black-and-white movie. It didn't matter which movie—there was something about that period of storytelling that soothed and calmed her.

"That's kind of you, but no, I…have plans." Regina knew the lie sounded clunky, but she couldn't possibly go.

"Oh, okay," Grace said. She picked up the half-drunk bubble tea from the desk. "I should actually get going anyway. I just remembered I said I'd make some calls this afternoon. Got to find out if I'll be moving next week."

"I hope you find somewhere nice and peaceful," Regina said.

Grace opened the door. "Anything will be more peaceful than where I am now! Have a great weekend."

"You, too." Regina watched Grace leave, wondering if she'd offended her by not taking her up on her offer. She hoped not, but if she had then maybe it was for the best. Putting some distance between them might be just what she needed.

She could still feel Grace's hand on her shoulder, despite the two layers separating skin from skin. The warm, comfortingly snug grip was something she wanted to feel again and again.

Being close to Grace equally excited and terrified her, something she needed to get under control. She resolved to not contact Grace that weekend at all, and if Grace contacted her, then she'd not reply immediately, even if that meant going for a long walk in the park and deliberately leaving her phone at home.

❖

Grace bumped into Crystal, one of the models from the evening-wear shoot, on her way out of Amandine.

"Oh, hey! I thought you left a while ago?" Crystal asked.

"I had to make a phone call, so I hung around here for a while," Grace fibbed.

"Not a good call, judging by the look on your face," Crystal said, obviously fishing.

Grace chuckled as they exited the building and walked side by side down the London street. She'd hoped that she didn't look as disappointed as she felt. But Regina's snub had hit her hard. She felt for sure they were getting closer, but then Regina seemed intent on keeping them apart again.

"There's a woman I'm interested in," Grace confessed, "and she's giving me such mixed signals. One minute I think she's interested, the next I think I'm dreaming it all. I just asked if she wanted to come out tonight with some friends and she turned me down. She said she had plans but...I don't know. It sounded a bit fake. I'm wondering if it might be a date. But then she would have said she had a date. I don't know. I just know that I feel as if she snubbed me."

Crystal nodded knowingly. "Been there. You wonder if you're losing your mind."

"Exactly. I just wished she'd say something if she wasn't

interested. But it's like there's a push and pull all the time. I see the way she looks at me, and I think she's interested. Then suddenly she's pulling away. I'm not sure what to do."

"Sounds like she's not worth it."

Grace chewed her lip. If the conversation was reversed, then she'd be giving Crystal exactly the same advice. But Grace knew that she was already invested. It wouldn't be easy to let go of the thoughts of pressing her lips to Regina's one day.

"I'm not ready to quit just yet," Grace said.

"Then you need to make it clear you're interested," Crystal suggested. "Make a move. Or at least make it really clear you want her to. Maybe she's not picking up on your signals."

"I don't know, I've been pretty blatant." Grace thought back to placing her hand on Regina's shoulder. She supposed that it could have been interpreted as an innocent move. "Maybe I do need to up the ante."

"Best to try. If it's making you miserable, then you need to know one way or another."

Grace nodded. "You're absolutely right."

"Of course I am. Let's grab a drink, and we can brainstorm some ideas." Crystal looped her arm through Grace's and pointed to a nearby bar. "Come on!"

CHAPTER FOURTEEN

After a full Saturday looking for new jobs, contemplating taking out a ridiculously priced loan, and investigating prices of apartments in a distant town in the North of England proclaimed online to be the cheapest place to live, Regina decided to spend Sunday with Bess.

It wasn't until she was halfway there that she thought to tell Bess she was on her way. Usually, she arrived unannounced without a thought. It wasn't as if Bess would be anywhere else. As time had marched on, Bess had become more and more reluctant to go out on her own. Not to mention that she didn't need to at Calm Acres. Everything she needed was on-site. Trips were organised by the management, and if Bess did fancy heading out, she could do so safe in the knowledge that she had the home bus available and staff watching out for her.

But with Leonard on the scene, there was a real possibility that Bess could be busy with her new boyfriend.

She called from the train, hoping that she hadn't made a wasted journey in her assumption that Bess would be as bored and lonely as she was. Thankfully, Bess was delighted to hear from her and even more pleased to hear Regina was planning to pop in.

When Regina arrived, Bess was waiting in reception. She leaned on her walking stick a little heavier than Regina remembered, a reminder that Bess was only going to get older. It was a horrible thought. Bess was all she had, and not having her around would be an adjustment to say the least.

They hugged in greeting and Bess gestured towards one of the public sitting rooms.

"Oh, I am glad to see you," Bess said once they were sitting down.

"How are things going with Leonard?" Regina asked, assuming that Bess's overly good mood was probably something to do with her new love and not an unexpected visit from her niece.

"He bought me flowers," Bess said. "And we're going to the cinema this evening."

Regina raised her eyebrow. Bess hadn't expressed interest in going to the cinema for as long as Regina could remember.

"Locally?" Regina asked, her worry clear.

Bess smiled. "Yes, just down the road. He's driving."

"And he's a good driver?"

"A very good driver," Bess said, reaching forward and placing a reassuring hand on Regina's knee. Ever since her parents had died, she'd seen danger lurking around every corner.

Regina nodded. "Okay. Well, that sounds nice. Although I didn't know you were interested in the cinema."

"I'm not usually," Bess mused. "It's funny how you look at things when you're seeing someone. I'm not someone to go to the cinema, or really go out much at all. But Leonard's always keeping busy, moving about from here to there and doing all sorts of things. He goes to a Pilates session two times a week. I'm going with him next week."

Regina just about managed to not allow her jaw to drop open. She'd been trying to convince Bess to do some form of activity for years. Pilates had been recommended following the knee operation, but Bess had firmly refused. But now Leonard had suggested it, and off she went.

She didn't say anything. She knew only too well what it was like. At the start of her relationship with Margot, she was frequently dragged along to things she didn't find of particular interest just because Margot said it would be fun. Of course, Margot's idea of fun didn't line up to Regina's, or even Leonard's.

"He's heading out to see his grandson today, but I asked him to pop by here to say hello to you before he left. I thought you'd want to vet him." Bess's eyes twinkled.

"I do," Regina agreed playfully.

"But you be nice."

"I'm always nice."

Bess made a face that said she didn't agree.

"You're all I have," Regina reminded her. "Excuse me if I'm a little overprotective sometimes."

"You should spend less time worrying about me and more time worrying about you. I don't want you to be alone like I've been."

Regina rolled her eyes and leaned back in her chair. She didn't need to hear this particular topic of conversation right now. Especially when she was trying to ignore a crush that had become all-consuming for her.

"Hello, ladies," a sprightly male voice called out.

Regina turned around. She wasn't sure what she was expecting, but he wasn't it. He was shorter than she'd thought he'd be, bald, and wore glasses. But what radiated from him was kindness and a smile that must have been permanently etched on his face if the laughter lines that marked his expression were anything to go by. She realised she'd been expecting to not like him, but there was not a chance that anyone wouldn't like this happy little man who practically bounded towards them.

They exchanged hellos, Leonard gallantly kissing Bess on the cheek as he stood beside her chair with a hand on her shoulder. It put her in mind of Grace a couple of days before.

"Bess tells me you are office-based?" Leonard asked.

"I am. I work in marketing," she replied, careful to not say too much. With every day that passed, it was becoming harder to tell Bess the truth.

"Marketing director," Bess added. She'd been so proud as Regina had ascended the career ladder.

"My daughter works in marketing," Leonard said. "She's a, let me get this right, media buyer? Is that the term?"

"It's a term I've heard of," Regina said.

"Well, let's assume that's the one." He chuckled. "I always

dread my family turning up and testing me on their job titles and companies. It's all changed since I was working."

"What did you do?" Regina asked.

"Operations director for an NHS trust," he said with a proud smile. "But that's managing the operations of the building, not managing operations as in chop chop."

Regina couldn't help but smile at the joke.

"Is Regina coming with us to the pictures tonight?" Leonard asked Bess, seemingly genuinely interested in the idea.

"I'm not certain," Bess said, looking to Regina. "Would you like to come?"

"That's kind of you, but I have plans," Regina said. "But thank you."

"Another time," Leonard promised. "I better get going. I'm off to see my grandson. He's a busy lad, but he's making some time for his grandpa today, so I don't want to keep him waiting. Don't be a stranger, Regina. I'd love for us to become good friends."

Regina found herself completely disarmed and thoroughly charmed. She could see what Bess saw in him. They said goodbye, Leonard kissing Bess on the cheek again and waving farewell to Regina before almost skipping from the room.

The second he was gone, Bess leaned forward and whispered, "What do you think?"

Regina was taken back to schooldays when she and her teenage friends would discuss boys.

"He seems very nice," Regina admitted.

Bess beamed. "He is." She sat back. "He really is."

Just like those teenage schooldays, Regina knew that she was about to be pushed aside for a boy. She didn't mind. Bess deserved a final chance at love. There had been a few men over the years but no one special. Regina wasn't unaware of how lonely Bess had found retirement and going into care. While she'd made plenty of friends, there had always been something missing.

"So, how is work?" Bess asked.

"Great," Regina lied. "We're all very busy, as usual."

"Will you be working Christmas Eve or will you be able to

come by? The local primary school are having the children come and sing carols for us."

Regina winced at the memory of the previous year's festivities. There wasn't a single child who could carry a tune, and the concert went on for forty-five long minutes.

"Elsie and me are going to crack open a good brandy and sit in the upstairs sitting room and take a wee sip every time someone sings off-key," Bess added. "It will be fun."

Regina laughed. "Well, in that case, I'll have to come because if they are anything like last year, you'll be drunk within ten minutes."

CHAPTER FIFTEEN

Monday came around, and Regina looked forward to another day of Margot being out of the office. She knew it would be a rarity and something to be enjoyed and not expected. A flurry of emails had come in from Margot over the weekend, but Regina steadfastly ignored them. Usually, she would have happily worked at the weekend in order to get a head start on the working week. But now she wanted to limit the time she interacted with Margot to as little as she could possibly manage.

She arrived bright and early and was surprised to see Arjun at his desk. So far, she'd always arrived before him and hoped that her own decision to start work early hadn't made him feel it necessary to do the same. Her lack of a private life shouldn't come at the cost of anyone else's.

"Good morning," she said. "You're in early today."

He nodded, a hint of tiredness on his face. "Yeah, couldn't sleep. Thought I'd get started early."

Regina could detect a hint of a lie underneath the comment, but she didn't know him well enough yet to question him. She wondered if she'd get the chance to get to know him or if she'd manage to escape Margot's clutches before then. She liked some parts of Amandine, such as the people, Margot aside. And the company had a good ethos for a clothing brand. But working with lingerie, models, and Margot made it somewhere she'd never have a future. If she ever did manage to get her gymnophobia under control, she couldn't imagine she'd ever be truly comfortable looking at half-naked bodies.

"If you want to head home early, that's fine with me," Regina told him. "I have a quiet afternoon."

Arjun looked contemplative before he nodded again. "Thanks, I might do that."

She entered her office and got some work done before preparing herself to head downstairs to the studio for that day's photo shoot. As much as she hated the photo shoot, she knew she'd also have the chance to see Grace.

A cloud had been hanging over her all weekend as she wondered whether she had offended Grace by turning down her invitation to go out with her friends. Even though she knew it was the right thing to do, she wanted to make sure things were still good between them. Maintaining boundaries and not tipping Grace off to her massive crush was one thing, but she didn't want to go too far and ruin the good friendship they had quickly built.

Arjun walked with her down to the studio. He updated her on her meetings that week, having liaised with Margot's office to rearrange Regina's calendar. She hated that her own assistant was now keenly aware that her boss felt the need to watch her every move. But if Arjun had any thoughts on the matter, he kept them to himself.

As they approached the studio, the door opened and Grace emerged. She was wearing a thick robe and sipping happily on some bubble tea.

"Hey, you two!" she said.

"Hey," Arjun said. He indicated the studio. "I'll go in and give Thomas those new notes."

"Good morning," Regina said. A weight lifted off her shoulders at seeing Grace's smiling face, seemingly none the worse after their Friday talk. "Did you have a nice weekend?"

"Yes, it was busy. How about you?"

"Quiet," Regina said. "I saw my aunt on Sunday."

"Did you meet her new man?"

Regina chuckled. "I did, actually. He's annoyingly lovely."

Grace laughed. "Why is that annoying?"

"Jealousy," Regina said, "pure and simple. I'm honestly delighted for my aunt, but it's hard to be single and hear about someone's perfect new love. I sound petty, I know."

"Not at all. I'd be the same. Besides, you can be happy for someone and still feel jealous. It's allowed. How was your Friday? You said you had plans. I assumed you had a date."

Regina had never been great at making up lies on the spot. Especially plausible ones. She hesitated a few moments before finally saying, "My shoes. I...I was cleaning out my shoes. Just me. No date."

Grace sipped her tea and looked perplexed. "I thought you said you had plans?"

"Well, I've been putting it off for ages. I had to do it Friday to...donate the ones I didn't want. To a charity shop. Who only open on Saturday mornings."

"Wow, it's amazing they stay open if they only open on Saturday mornings," Grace commented.

"Isn't it?" Regina indicated the studio door. "Are you joining us?"

"I'm just heading out to make a quick phone call. My agent found a new place for me. I'm super excited! I saw it on Sunday and it's so cute—it's available now, so I want to grab it and get moved in. Completely new area for me as well, closer to town."

"Oh, that's wonderful. I hope you get it. I'll see you in there." Regina put her hand on the door plate, hoping to get away from Grace and give herself a stern talking-to about making up plausible lies.

Grace placed her hand on Regina's forearm. "While we're alone..."

Regina paused. She turned to look at Grace, wishing that her heart would stop thudding against her ribcage every time she gazed at those perfect features.

"Do you want me to come to your office this afternoon? To go through this photo shoot? I don't want to overstep—"

"I'd love your help," Regina interjected. As much as she'd love to be able to review the photos from the shoot on her own, she knew she'd be lost without Grace's patient tutelage.

Grace could tell when Regina was becoming overwhelmed by the images and would minimise the photo on the screen and change the topic of conversation for a while. She'd highlight images she thought needed work, blitz through ones that didn't need comments and could simply be approved.

If Regina had to manage on her own, it would take her many hours and a few glasses of wine to get through just one shoot. Not only did Grace help her through the difficulties in looking at the contents of the photos, but she also had an excellent eye for detail. Regina would be mad to not seek out her advice.

Grace beamed. "Usual time?"

"Absolutely," Regina agreed.

❖

Regina sat in her office and cupped her mug of tea, relishing the warmth and comfort it provided. She'd made it herself in the office kitchen to demonstrate to Arjun that she was perfectly capable of making herself a drink after he had brought her multiple hot drinks throughout the day.

She couldn't blame him. They were close enough now that he could tell when something was wrong. He might not have understood why she was out of sorts during the photo shoot, but he'd obviously picked up on something. Cups of tea, softly spoken comments about missed calls and rescheduled meetings, and a permanent frown on his face had spoken volumes of Arjun's concern.

She imagined it wouldn't be long before he put two and two together and worked out that she had an issue with the photo shoots, specifically an issue with the skin on display. If he hadn't already.

She picked up her phone and called Arjun to pop into the office.

A moment later, he appeared with a notepad in hand.

"You won't need that," she assured him. "I just wanted to say I was serious about my offer earlier if you wanted to go home early. It's been a long day, and you're not paid enough to work these hours."

"I…" He hesitated. "I had a row with my girlfriend."

Regina had suspected something was up. "I'm sorry to hear that."

He shrugged, pretending that it didn't matter much to him, but his heart was on his sleeve and indicated that it did.

"Do you want to fix it?"

He blinked, clearly surprised at Regina's directness. "Yes."

"That's the most important thing," Regina said. She put her mug of tea on the coaster and sat forward. "I find most things resolve themselves when both parties want to fix the situation."

"It was just a silly argument about who takes the bin out." He stuck his hands in his pockets. "It's a man's job, but the smell of the bin actually makes me gag. Like, I've been properly sick before."

Regina rolled her eyes at the term *man's job*. "Does she know that?"

"No…well, I said I don't like it. But she doesn't like it either. So we leave it to overflow, and then whoever has the straw that breaks the camel's back has to do it."

"You have to tell her how much you dislike it, otherwise how will she know? You can't keep that to yourself."

"It's just so stupid."

"No, Arjun, it's life. Unfortunately, some of us find what other people think of simple tasks completely impossible. Do you love her?"

"Yes, of course."

"Then be honest with her. What's her name?"

"Maya."

"Then you say to her, *Maya, I'm sorry about the bin situation. I didn't want to tell you but the smell of the bin makes me feel ill, not just a little but like I'm going to be physically sick. I didn't want to tell you because of toxic masculinity.*"

Arjun grinned at the joke.

Regina smiled and continued, "Apologise for not telling

her sooner and explain to her exactly how bad the problem is. If she's worth your time, she'll understand, and you'll figure out a compromise. Maybe a peg for your nose."

He grimaced. "I'll talk to her and I'll tell her. But I'm not sure about the peg. We have communal bins outside the flat, and I'm not sure my neighbours will understand."

Regina shrugged playfully. "A solution's a solution. Now, off you go."

"Now?" He looked panicked.

She looked at her wristwatch. "Yes, might as well."

"Sh-she's at work."

"Well, be all romantic and meet her from work," Regina said, becoming a little exasperated. "Good Lord, come on, Arjun. Go and fix things, or you'll be in here again first thing tomorrow morning with me, and neither of us wants that."

He grinned from ear to ear. "Okay, yes, you're right. I'll…I'll be off, then."

"At last," she teased. "Good luck and see you tomorrow."

"See you tomorrow. And thanks." He darted out of the room, filled with what Regina hoped was enthusiasm that would last all the way to Maya's place of work.

It wasn't lost on her that advising others on their romantic situations came a lot easier to her than her own love life. She'd never had the confidence to flirt or make the first move, which she knew in her heart had led to a string of poorly matched relationships.

To take her mind off things, she dove into work. She was comfortable with the planning part of her job. She could build the marketing campaign, plan budgets, and predict income like the best in her field. She just wished it was any other product.

Time got away from her, and a knock on the door shook her from her thoughts.

Grace stood there with a drink in each hand. "Am I interrupting?"

"Yes. But please do," Regina said. She gestured to the chair in front of her desk.

Grace's expression burst into a smile and she placed the drinks on the desk before closing the office door.

"Where's Arjun?"

"He's, um, headed off early," Regina said. Her gaze had faltered when she'd noticed that Grace was wearing a zip-top hoodie, zipped up to just above her breasts and apparently with nothing underneath. Certainly nothing Regina could see.

Regina could never imagine wearing something where just a zip was all that protected her modesty. But that was one of the major differences between her and Grace. Grace was comfortable in her body.

Grace sat down and picked up her drink and took a long sip through the straw.

"Did you speak with your agent about your new place?" Regina asked.

"Yes, I'm moving this week. He's being a sweetheart and arranging the movers and everything. I have back-to-back jobs, and I can't let people down."

Regina wished she had an agent to help her when she next decided to move. She remembered when she'd moved into her apartment and what a shambles it had been with the mover turning up two hours later than expected and the packing took far longer than she had thought. Having an agent to worry about such things would have been nice.

"That's good. I certainly am happy to hear that," Regina said. "Before we start on the photos from today's shoot, I was wondering if we could pick up on my question from last week. Plunge bras and balcony bras? Margot is certainly going to quiz me when she's back. I tried to look it up online, but, well, a visual comparison wasn't very helpful."

"Sure," Grace said happily. "Balcony bras and balconettes are usually underwired and have less all-over cover, so they are great for low neckline tops. Plunge are similar but they have a much deeper V-neckline, the wires are shorter, too, and they squeeze to give more oomph."

"So they are both for low neckline clothes?" Regina asked, getting confused.

"Yes, but they're different." Grace got her mobile phone out and swiped and jabbed at the screen. "Balcony is lifting the boobs. Like an actual balcony, but instead of a person standing on the balcony, it's boobs."

Not sure how to react, Regina laughed.

Grace joined in. "Okay, maybe that description isn't helpful. I have an image here, but I've zoomed in so you should be okay."

She placed her phone on the table and slid it towards Regina. A close up of someone, Regina wondered if it was Grace, wearing a deep purple bra filled the screen. "Do you see what I mean? Not fully covering my—I mean *the* boobs."

Regina swallowed and nodded. "I see. Yes. But what makes this different to a plunge bra?"

Grace took the phone again and carried on swiping and jabbing the screen. "I can't find the one I'm looking for. Plunge is like, more oomph, deeper. Like, they are similar but..." Grace was clearly becoming frustrated at not being able to find the words she wanted or a picture to demonstrate. Regina almost regretted asking and causing Grace distress, but she needed to know if she was going to be able to do her job.

❖

Grace knew what she wanted to do. She also knew it would probably be a very bad idea. Regina's gymnophobia was something she needed to take seriously. While they had come along in leaps and bounds recently, that had been because of Grace's patience and understanding of Regina's boundaries.

While she had at one point briefly thought that immersion therapy and ripping the Band-Aid off might have been a good idea, she now knew better. Regina's bright red cheeks, shortness of breath, and averting of eyes all told her that Regina needed time and space to adjust to any kind of nudity.

But now Regina was asking an important question, and Grace knew there was only one way to explain the difference between the two garments. Without the photo she needed, there was only one other way to demonstrate. And, if she was brutally honest with herself, she had worn her outfit with the hope that she might be able to read more into whether Regina might have any romantic feelings towards her.

She stood up and tossed the phone down on her chair. She took the zip of her hoodie and pulled it down. "I'm sorry, but I can't think of a better way to describe it. This is a plunge bra."

Regina's eyes widened in something that looked like horror "I…see."

Grace was thankful that she had Regina's attention and she hadn't immediately looked away or run out of the room. Trying to maintain an air of professionalism, she pointed to the middle of her bra.

"There's no underwire here, to allow them to push together. No underwire means less material, and more of a dip for low-cut tops, but also pushing them together to make more of them. See?"

Regina clearly had no choice but to stare right at Grace's chest. And stare she did. Grace didn't know if Regina had short-circuited, was learning about plunge and balcony bras, or was interested in what she saw.

Grace tilted to the side. "And more material here." She pointed to the side of her breast, just below her armpit.

"O-okay," Regina half stuttered and half squeaked. "Good to, um, know. Thank you."

Grace was no closer to knowing what was going on in Regina's head, but she knew she couldn't torment the woman any longer. She zipped up her hoodie but cheekily decided to leave it a little more open than it had been when she'd arrived. She didn't like to toy with Regina, but she also hated not knowing how Regina felt about her.

She felt a little guilty for stripping off in front of Regina like that, but she honestly didn't have any other plan of action in the heat of the moment. The answer to the question was right there under her hoodie.

"I'm sorry, I just get frustrated when I can't find the right words. And this just felt quicker. I'm sorry," Grace said.

"It's fine." Regina's face gave her away.

It wasn't fine. She wasn't fine. But Grace still didn't know if it was because she was uncomfortable with nudity or if she was interested in Grace. Both fitted Regina's reaction.

"You did great, you didn't go nearly as red as you usually do," Grace said.

Regina chuckled. "Thank you. Maybe this exposure therapy is working. I still don't know how you can just…show yourself like that. You don't feel shy or exposed?"

Grace moved her phone from the chair and sat down. "Maybe a few times. When I worked with men who openly objectified me or when I worked with women who criticised my body."

"Women criticise your body?" Regina sounded scandalised at the thought.

"Sure. All the time. Often women are harder on other women than men are. You get used to stuff like that. It's just work. The clothes are just a product for sale. I'm just showing them. Nothing more."

Regina didn't look like she agreed. Grace had never worried much about what other people thought of her body. She'd heard it all, the good, the bad, and the indifferent. But she was impatient to know if Regina found her attractive. She needed some room to breathe or she might just come out and ask and potentially ruin the friendship they had developed.

"I'm just going to pop to the kitchen and get some water. Do you want anything?"

"No, thank you." Regina picked up the takeaway tea that Grace had brought in with her and took a fortifying sip.

Grace glided from the room with as much casualness as she could muster. But inside she felt confused. She felt for sure that she had seen indicators of interest coming from Regina. A wistful look, a gaze that lasted a little too long, a seemingly unconscious licking of her lips. And yet, nothing ever happened.

Was she being rejected or not? Did Regina maybe think she was too young? Was she not interested in models? Or did Regina simply find her unattractive?

Any or all were possible.

The problem was that Grace's initial romantic interest in

Regina had morphed into so much more. Regina was fast becoming an important friend. Someone Grace didn't want to lose. It was an increasingly difficult line to walk.

❖

The lines between Regina's general discomfort with nudity and her concern around Grace discovering her crush were colliding. She no longer knew where one ended and the other began. Saying something would be impossible—she barely knew how she felt herself and wouldn't be able to explain it to anyone else, and certainly not to Grace.

Grace returned to the office with a glass of water and a plate. "I found Hobnobs," she whispered gleefully. "I haven't had Hobnobs for years. They are my faves. Jenn said they were plated up for a meeting, but no one ate them. So we have to eat them, or they'll be thrown away."

Regina chuckled. "We?"

"Yes, you're going to be an accomplice in this biscuit destruction."

Grace dragged her chair around the desk to Regina's as she always did when they worked together. Once she sat down, she picked up a Hobnob and bit into it, moaning as she did.

"They are just so good," she said in between chews. "Have one."

Regina picked up a biscuit and broke it in half and ate a small piece. She didn't mind Hobnobs but also didn't consider them a gastronomic delight as Grace seemed to.

Grace rolled her eyes at Regina's delicate little nibble.

Regina opened the laptop and accessed the photo shoot gallery for that day. Grace leaned forward and said, "Right, let's see what we have here."

She took another bite of biscuit, and Regina watched as a small piece of the oaty, crumbly snack fell from her lips and landed between her breasts. Regina looked from the biscuit piece to Grace's face and back again. Grace seemed utterly unaware of the situation.

"Um. You have…There's some…"

Grace looked at her, and Regina immediately looked towards the ceiling, trying to make it look like she hadn't been staring at Grace's chest.

"Some…?" Grace asked, clearly perplexed.

Regina meant to point in the general direction of Grace's chest, but with her eyes skyward and never having had much spatial awareness, she instead plunged her hand right into the open hoodie. The shock of what had happened made her look at her hand and its completely inappropriate and unplanned location.

At that moment, the door flung open, and Margot stormed in. She'd clearly been in a rage before she entered and now looked like she might actually explode.

Regina snatched her hand back.

"It's a bit of Hobnob," she said, defensively.

Chapter Sixteen

Margot stared at Regina in a way that made Regina believe in and start to worry about spontaneous human combustion. Regina wondered how on earth she'd managed to get herself into such a predicament and how Grace's skin could feel so soft.

"So, this is why you pushed me away," Margot said knowingly. "You're sleeping with her."

"What? No." Regina stood up and looked from Margot to Grace and back in shock horror. "No, of course I'm not sleeping with Grace. There's nothing between us—don't be foolish, Margot."

Margot gave a caustic laugh. "Oh, sure. I'm being foolish, when you're in here, with your door closed and your assistant nowhere to be seen, a hand in her bra. Is this a midlife crisis? Some ridiculous desire to bed a young underwear model?" Margot sneered at Grace. "Well…youngish."

Regina felt her cheeks heat up with outrage and embarrassment. She couldn't look at Grace for fear of what she must think of Margot's outburst and the tiny hint of truth that laced her words.

Grace jumped out of her chair. "I'll leave you two to talk," she mumbled before Regina could say a word.

"Why on earth did you say that?" Regina snapped at Margot.

Margot smirked. "Which bit?"

"All of it. I'm not sleeping with her, but even if I was it wouldn't be because of a midlife crisis or some need to…to prove something." Regina flopped into her chair. She thought the statement said a lot more about Margot than it did her.

"What was she doing here then?" Margot folded her arms.

"We were talking. She's a friend. Nothing more." Regina wasn't about to admit to the help Grace had been offering her with work.

Margot scoffed. "Girls like her are not friends with women like you."

Regina rolled her eyes. "Grace is a woman. She's in her thirties." She paused as she caught on to Margot's comment. "What do you mean women like me?"

Margot sighed as if preparing herself to try and explain a very simple concept to a small child. "You're predictable, Regina, with your quiet, simple, safe, and predictable life."

"So what?"

Margot's expression softened slightly. "I say this with great affection, but you're terribly dull. Which is fine, it's something I've even grown to like. It's sweet. But it's not a trait that famous and unfairly attractive people would enjoy."

Regina started to open her mouth to issue a swift rebuttal but found she couldn't. It was true. She was dull. She'd always known it, and she herself had been surprised at Grace's desire to spend any time with her.

"If Grace is spending time with you," Margot continued, "it's probably for professional gain. Nothing more. Stay away from her."

Regina didn't believe it. She knew honest friendship when she saw it. Margot wouldn't recognise it because she only ever chewed up and spat out everyone she ever met. Yes, Grace had wanted advice, but she'd also given advice. And beyond that, they'd talked, laughed, shared stories, and bonded.

"I don't want to stay away from her," Regina said. "But not for the reasons you think. We are friends. Nothing more."

"I forbid it," Margot said. "You're not to see her."

Regina's jaw fell open. She shook her head and quickly started to pack away her laptop. "I'm not having this conversation with you, Margot. I'm going home for the day. You don't get to order me about like this. I'm a person. Honestly, I can't believe I actually dated you. Actually, I can. Because this isn't you at all—you've changed. To be honest, I'm worried about you."

Margot's face morphed into an ugly sort of smile. "It's because, on some level, you still love me."

Regina shook her head in despair. She pulled the strap of her laptop bag over her shoulder and started to leave.

Margot grabbed her arm. "Regina, don't go after her."

"Carry on like this, and I'll report you to HR," Regina promised.

"You won't." Margot sneered. "We both know your financial situation. You need this job to keep that ancient aunt of yours in that home you pay for."

Regina gritted her teeth. Damn Margot for knowing which buttons to press.

"No more groping models," Margot said. "Either in here or anywhere else."

"I wasn't groping—" Regina stopped when Margot's grip on her arm tightened. "I'm not coming back to you, Margot. I want that to be very, very clear. If you're planning to blackmail me into continuing our toxic relationship, think again."

Margot loosened her grip. "I'm not desperate enough to blackmail anyone. If you're not ready, that's absolutely fine. You'll come around soon enough, I'm sure."

Regina decided not to respond. Margot was clearly losing it, and Regina wasn't about to make matters worse for herself. She needed to get out of the office and weigh up her options carefully.

"I mean what I say," Margot continued. "No more seeing Grace Holland. Don't think I haven't seen how you look at her. If you continue to see her, then I'll tell HR that you're in an inappropriate relationship with one of the models."

Regina narrowed her eyes. Margot's jealousy could be seen from space. As much as Regina hated Margot's ridiculous power plays, she knew she couldn't escape from the fact that Margot did hold all the cards here. Regina needed the job, and she agreed it looked bad to be hanging out with Grace even if nothing was happening. No one would believe her, not once Margot started spinning her web of lies.

"And how am I supposed to do my job?" Regina asked. "Because you're the one who wants me to attend the photo shoots, Margot."

"You'll attend them, but you'll have nothing else to do with Grace Holland. You'll thank me for it, trust me. These younger women think they own the world. Just because society puts so much value in wrinkle-free skin and tiny waists."

For the first time, Regina seriously started to wonder if Margot's mercurial mood wasn't simply because she'd been dumped. There was a real possibility that she was also navigating some sort of midlife crisis. She'd clearly had some kind of cosmetic work done since Regina had last seen her, and working in the fashion industry didn't seem to be doing much for her mental health.

"Real beauty is ageless," Regina said. "I think we women in our forties are in our prime. It's not like it was twenty years ago. Not now. The world has changed."

Margot sneered.

"I mean it," Regina insisted. "I know I'm not alone in thinking that laugh lines are a beautiful sign of someone who lives a happy life. Glittering streams of silver in hair are so coveted that many women dye their hair to get the effect. And personality-wise, we're often calmer and more confident." She looked Margot in the eye. "I'm not dating Grace. But if I was, it wouldn't be because of her age. Or because she's a model. I don't care about such things, and if you think I do, then that proves how little you ever really knew me."

"Oh, I know you're not dating her," Margot said. She started to leave, pausing at the door to deliver her parting words, "Because if you do, I'll ruin you."

She stormed away, heels slamming into the thin office carpet in a way that would certainly leave damage. Regina let out a sigh and hung her head in despair. She needed a new job before this one tore her apart.

Chapter Seventeen

Regina looked at the screen, hung up the call, and hit the redial button. She'd done the same thing five times since she'd started walking home. Each of her calls to Grace went unanswered, eventually ticking over to an automated voicemail service.

She couldn't blame Grace for not wanting to speak with her. She couldn't imagine what Grace must be thinking after Margot's explosion. But Regina needed to speak with her. She needed to apologise for putting Grace in the line of Margot's fire in the first, and then explain the tricky situation she was now placed in which meant she'd no longer be able to spend time with Grace.

As much as she hated it, Margot held the cards, and if she said she'd make Regina's life a living nightmare if she saw Regina and Grace together, then she meant it.

The call, like the others, connected to voicemail. Regina hung up. She wasn't about to leave a personality-less voicemail when the situation was so important. In fact, if she had her preference, then she'd see Grace face to face for the conversation. One last personal encounter to try to explain the ludicrous situation Regina found herself in and say a heartfelt sorry for unwittingly dragging Grace into the nightmare.

She gripped her phone tightly. Her pace had quickened with her frustration. At this rate, she'd be home in no time. Not that she found that thought particularly comforting. She was on edge and in need of venting but with no one to vent to.

Bess came to mind. She regretted not telling Bess of her

employment situation from the start. If she had, then she'd be able to talk to her now. Bess had always been a straight talker, enough heart to understand the difficult nuances of certain situations, but also practical and balanced. Regina missed her advice.

There was one way to get that advice, she reminded herself.

She sucked in a quick breath and called Bess before her nerves left her.

"Hello, poppet," Bess answered after the usual half a dozen rings.

"Hi," Regina said. While she was relieved to be speaking with the one person she knew she could talk to about anything, she was aware her tone sounded like she'd dropped a fifty pound note down a drain while stopping to opportunistically pick up an abandoned pound coin.

"Oh dear," Bess said immediately, "I know that sigh. Something's up. What's wrong?"

"It's just...work," Regina said, suddenly losing her nerve. There were reasons why she hadn't told Bess everything. Good reasons. She'd felt as though she was protecting Bess by keeping secrets. Now it felt like the going had gotten too tough, and she was breaking that promise with herself through her own weakness.

"Just work." Bess huffed. "Honestly, you're as bad a liar as my little brother was."

Regina smiled to herself. She was a terrible liar, just like her father had been. Maybe she'd called Bess knowing that and knowing that she'd be forced to confess her secrets.

"It is a work thing that's also a personal thing," Regina said, knowing she was skirting around the edge of the topic until she had some courage to finally dive in and come clean.

"Well, I have a fresh cup of tea, and I'm sitting down. Tell your nosy old aunt everything, and we'll see if it warrants that sigh of yours."

Regina smiled to herself. This was what she wanted. What she needed. Even if it went against her better judgement of protecting Bess from the truth, it was the right thing to do.

"Do you remember I used to be in a relationship with Margot?" Regina asked.

Bess sucked in a sharp breath. "Oh, Regina. Not her again. Please, tell me you're not dating that shrew again."

Regina laughed. "No, I'm not dating her."

"Thank heavens. You spent a long time trying to extract yourself from that situation. You need to stay as far away from that controlling woman as possible."

Regina blew out a silent breath. "Well. That's going to be tricky."

"Tell me everything," Bess said. There was no judgement in her tone, which Regina was grateful for.

Bess had hated Margot but had always been fair-minded when talking about her. At first, Regina wasn't sure if she'd stay in the relationship, in the good old days when Margot's behaviour was slightly questionable but not outright controlling. Bess had listened and allowed Regina to come to her own conclusions. When Regina had finally ended things, Bess had nodded and admitted that she'd found Margot to be a horrible shrew.

Initially, Regina had been irritated that Bess hadn't spoken up and told Regina her real thoughts on Margot from the start. But when Regina realised that Bess was allowing her to come to her own conclusion and make her own unbiased decisions, she understood.

"I no longer work for Precision Marketing," Regina said. "Peter took out a loan, essentially bankrupting the company. No one saw it coming."

"Oh my. Why didn't you tell me, poppet?"

Regina bit her lip. "I didn't want to worry you."

"Seems a silly thing to do. You know you can talk to me about anything."

"I know. I just felt…" Regina was struck by the realisation for the first time. "I felt guilty."

"Why guilty? Did you make Peter take out the loan?"

"No."

"Did you push the company into bankruptcy? Buying too many

of those mechanical pencil things you love so much? Although why a normal pencil won't do is beyond me."

Regina chuckled. "No. I felt guilty because my financial situation directly impacts yours."

"Then it should be me who feels guilty, not you," Bess said.

"No, you shouldn't. You gave me everything when I was growing up. You never made me feel I needed to worry about having a roof over my head, food on the table, or having money. I felt safe and secure. It wasn't until I was older that I realised what a blessing that was. And I wanted to give that back to you."

Regina had known that deep down, but verbalising her feelings somehow hit her differently. The need to protect Bess from the truth was a direct result of Bess's ability to protect Regina at a time when she'd lost everything.

"You don't owe me anything," Bess said firmly. "Would you have loved me any less if we'd struggled for money? No. Our bond is beyond that. We love each other no matter what. All I need to know is if I need to pack my things?"

"No, absolutely not. I've got another job. For now. It's just… It's tricky."

"I'm assuming we're about to get to the Margot part of this story?"

"Yes. After I realised I was out of a job, I started applying for jobs. There were precious few around at my level. I spoke to recruitment consultants who said the market was quiet at the moment. I posted on LinkedIn—do you know what that is?"

"I've heard of it, but I don't know what it is."

"It's a social media platform but for the business part of your life. Facebook for business, sort of."

"People post pictures of their sandwiches at work rather than at home?" Bess chuckled to herself. She'd been firmly anti–social media since the day Regina had shown her a platform and she'd spotted someone posting pictures of a terrible-looking meal they had cooked.

"Sort of," Regina agreed, not wanting to be drawn into a long conversation about the pros and cons of social media. "Margot saw my post, but I didn't know that. Someone had dropped out of a role at her company at the last minute, and she was desperately looking for someone to replace them. It was a bit of an opportunity for her to kill two birds with one stone. Fill the role and…torment me. Everything went through the HR department. I didn't know I worked for her until my first day."

"Sounds like something she'd do," Bess huffed.

"And the job…I can do it. It's just…"

"Just?"

"I work for Amandine."

"Where do I know that name? Oh, the clothing brand?"

"That's them. They are launching a new line, and that's what I'm in charge of, marketing the new line."

"What are you not telling me?" Bess asked.

Regina felt her face heat up at just the thought of it. Now that she was laying out the details for Bess, her understanding of Margot's manipulation was greater. From the centre of the storm, it was difficult to see just how hard the rain was falling.

"It's a lingerie line."

"But surely she knows—"

"She knows," Regina confirmed. "She's made it clear she wants me to suffer. She's also made it clear she wants me to date her again. Well, I think she thinks I'll fall in love with her."

"You have to leave that job."

"I can't."

"I'll find somewhere to live, don't you worry. I'm old, we have a national health service, they won't leave me out on the streets. There's no reason for you to suffer for me, Regina. None at all."

"There's more to it." Regina hated that she'd managed to get herself into such a dilemma.

"Go on," Bess said at the prolonged silence that followed.

"My industry, the marketing industry, often announces when people take on new roles. Especially if they are marketing opportunities in themselves. So, Amandine want everyone to know that they are branching out into new fashion ranges. A way to do that is to announce a new person working for the company to do that. Every little helps, when it comes to marketing. So, the day I started, Margot arranged for an announcement to be sent out to tell the industry that I now work for Amandine. If I leave after such a short amount of time, it will look very bad."

"You mean you might not be able to get another job?" Bess clarified.

"Exactly. This sort of thing can break careers. I remember a woman who started at an investment bank and left a week later. The assumption was that she couldn't handle the pressure. No one wanted to take a risk on her, not knowing why she left and with rumours swirling. I've no idea what happened to her. But I know she doesn't have a top job in marketing anymore."

"What do you think Margot's plan is?"

Regina realised that she'd arrived outside her apartment and wondered if she'd managed some sort of record. She was so swept up in what had happened and her call to Bess that she could hardly recall any of the journey home.

"I don't know," she admitted. "She seems…unstable. And I say that in a kind way. I'm worried about her."

"Don't waste your pity on someone who is treating you this way," Bess said, uncharacteristically harsh.

"You taught me to care about people. Even people like Margot."

Bess sighed. "I suppose I did."

"This afternoon she really seemed…unhinged," Regina said. "I was in my office with a model, Grace, and she snapped."

"Why?"

Regina thought about the situation Margot walked in on. A Hobnob biscuit in a bra, Regina trying to look away and point at the crumb at the same time. It was a full-on farce. And Bess would laugh her socks off if Regina admitted to it.

"She thought we were in a relationship," she said.

"Why did she jump to that conclusion?"

Regina let herself into her apartment and placed her laptop bag on the floor. She headed to the kitchen and picked up a bottle of red wine from the wine rack.

"I've been helping Grace, and she's been helping me. She wants advice on how to break into marketing, and I need someone's expert eyes on the photo shoots for the new line. We've sort of become friends while we've worked. Margot didn't like that idea. She immediately assumed that we were"—she hesitated to say exactly what Margot had said—"together. And barred me from seeing Grace again. Which I don't want to do, because I like her and she's the only person I really connected with at Amandine."

"She barred you from seeing someone? Oh, Regina, that's a... What do they call them these days? Oh yes, a red flag."

"I know."

"Margot is one big red flag."

"I know that, too," Regina said. She shouldered the phone and poured herself half a glass of wine. "So now I need to apologise to Grace."

"I know you think it will ruin your career, but I still think you should leave. Work isn't everything," Bess said.

"I need the money. I can tough this out for a while, until something else comes up. I'm registered with every recruitment agency in London. If anything comes up, they'll be in touch."

"You mean I need the money. I'm not unaware of the cost of this place. If you didn't have me to worry about, you'd be able to leave. Am I right?"

"No. I have my own bills, too," Regina said.

"I can tell when you're lying."

"I don't want you to leave Calm Acres," Regina said. "You're happy and settled. And you just met Leonard."

"I'd be moving, not dying. And you shouldn't give up a friendship because your ex is clearly jealous. Besides, the way you say Grace's name makes me think there's more there than you're admitting to."

Regina drank some wine and wondered how she was so transparent to Bess, even over the phone. She hoped it was only to Bess.

"There's nothing there," Regina said.

"But you want there to be?"

Regina laughed. She hoped it sounded casual and not as forced as it actually was.

"She's in her early thirties and a model. We have nothing in common."

Bess sniggered.

"What's so funny?"

"Nothing. You're just as transparent as your father. You've not denied anything, poppet. Do you like her?"

Regina took her wine glass into the living room and sat down on the sofa. She swirled the glass and watched the liquid lap at the sides.

"Not that it's relevant or even remotely possible, even with the whole Margot situation to one side. But, yes. I do like her."

There. She'd said it out loud. An invisible weight lifted from her shoulders. Of course, she'd known that she felt that way towards Grace. But there was something so real in saying it.

"Then leave that job, and tell her you like her. Who knows what might happen?"

Regina rolled her eyes. Lovestruck Aunt Bess was not as pragmatic as lonely Aunt Bess who had gone before her.

"I know what will happen. Grace won't be interested in me, I won't be able to find another job, and you'd be out of Calm Acres and end up God knows where."

"Or she might say yes and that she was waiting for you to get the courage up to ask her out. You're too negative, poppet."

"Realistic," Regina corrected.

"It's ultimately your decision, of course," Bess said. "But I hope you decide to take a risk. I know you think you have everything figured out, but sometimes life can surprise you. Sometimes things work out, even when we can't see how it can possibly happen."

"I'll stick with Amandine for a while longer and see what comes up. I'm okay where I am. I can handle Margot, and I'm getting there with the job. It's work, and it's a steady income." Regina took a sip of wine. She'd been telling herself those two facts on repeat every time she had a tough moment at work.

"Don't struggle on for me, poppet. Really. I can figure things out."

"Promise me you won't do anything. No packing your things. Or making any calls," Regina pleaded. "Just stay put and don't try to help me with this. Please?"

"I'll not do a thing. But know that I happily will if you need me to."

"Noted." Regina sat back. "Do you have any nice news to brighten my evening?"

"Actually, I do. Leonard's grandson is coming by to see us. Apparently, he's as big a *Frost* fan as I am."

Regina smiled at the memories of watching episodes of the detective series with Bess over the years. When they'd all come out on DVD, Bess had acted like a lottery winner. The perfect evening, as far as Bess was concerned, was a couple of episodes of *A Touch of Frost* with some salty snacks and a little bit of whisky to wash it all down. Regina used those evenings as opportunities to catch up on some sleep, cuddling into the giant cushions Bess had on her sofa and catnapping to the dialogue she practically knew by heart.

"He says he streams the episodes, but when I told him I have the behind the scenes specials and the bloopers, well, he said he couldn't wait to come over. The three of us are going to get a pizza delivered."

Regina smiled. It wasn't much, but it was also perfection.

"You should join us!" Bess sounded excited at the prospect, unsurprising since *Frost* and pizza were her favourite things, and sharing them with more people would just enhance the experience in her mind.

"No. I appreciate the offer, but I'm not the best of company at the moment," Regina said.

"Well, if you change your mind, you let me know. There is always a place here for you. Always."

Regina pulled her legs onto the sofa and pulled the blanket off the back pillows. She snuggled into the fabric. "So, tell me more about Leonard."

She could almost hear Bess beaming through the phone, and she launched into a story about the funny things he had said. Regina cradled her wine glass and listened to the soothing tales, temporarily ignoring her problems. They could wait until the morning.

CHAPTER EIGHTEEN

Grace finally returned Regina's multiple calls the following morning as she walked to work. Regina nearly dropped her phone in her hurry to answer.

"Grace, thank you so much for returning my call."

"I'm sorry I didn't call you last night," Grace said, her voice so small it caused Regina to turn up the volume on her phone.

"That's fine. Perfectly understandable. Are you okay?"

"I guess. I mean, it's not my first altercation with Margot. But she's never been that venomous to my face. I had to get out of there—sorry I ran away and left you to it. I should have probably stayed and backed you up."

Regina couldn't help but smile at Grace's sweet nature. Anyone with any common sense would have run away from Margot on the warpath. Even the suggestion of staying when Margot's anger was in full swing was an extraordinary kindness.

"You did the right thing to leave," Regina assured her. "She's worse than I've ever seen her. And I broke up with her once."

"I'm still surprised to think of you two together," Grace said, her voice still soft.

"It surprises me, too. She was very different then. I'm not sure what's happened to her. Not that I'm defending her. She's out of control and her behaviour is unacceptable. I'm sorry for what she said to you."

"You don't need to apologise for her behaviour."

"No, I suppose I don't. But she won't, and I imagine it hurt you greatly, so I will. It's my fault she caught us in that compromising position." She was glad for the cold November wind blowing against her cheeks. They were already red raw, and so the rush of blood that just flooded her cheeks wasn't going to make much difference.

Grace chuckled. It wasn't her usual laughter, just a small murmur. "Yeah. I found the bit of biscuit. Thank you for that."

Regina pushed the thought of the feeling of Grace's soft skin far away. She couldn't get off topic now. She needed to tell Grace what had happened after she'd left. She needed to explain Margot's threat and the consequences, which had kept her awake most of the night. Knowing she had to stay away from Grace was one thing—finding the situation wholly unfair was another.

"I'm afraid Margot went on a bit of a rampage after you left," Regina continued. "She's convinced that we're seeing each other. She's demanded that stop."

"We're not seeing each other. You made that very clear."

Regina paused. She was sure she could detect a tone in Grace's voice, but without visual cues and with her voice being so soft, it was difficult to be certain.

"She didn't believe me," Regina said. "She's demanded that we don't see each other. At all."

"Oh."

The single word hung between them for a while before Regina realised she'd have to carry on speaking. "Obviously, I can't argue with her. She jumped from accusing you of using me for your own gains, to me using my position of authority over you inappropriately. She can't be reasoned with."

"I'm not using you—"

"I know," Regina said. "I absolutely know that. We're friends, nothing more. But Margot can't see that. And she holds all the cards. I need this job, and she even brought up my aunt's care home."

"She really is despicable," Grace muttered.

"She is." Regina wasn't about to defend Margot, even if she was convinced there was a lot more to her behaviour of late. "I'm so sorry, this does mean that we can't see each other. Outside of the photo shoots, of course."

"How will you cope with checking the photos?" Grace asked.

Regina couldn't believe how sweet she was, caring more about Regina's difficult situation than anything else. How Margot couldn't see that this person wasn't a user was beyond Regina. Anyone who took the time to get to know Grace would clearly find nothing but selflessness and kindness.

"I'll muddle through. I have some coping techniques now that a good friend taught me. I'm just sorry that I won't be able to help you with your career change questions. Or to just talk. I really will miss our time together."

"Hopefully, you'll find a new job and get out from under Margot's control, and we'll have those times again," Grace said. "I better go. Hair and make-up need to see me. See you shortly."

Grace ended the call. Regina wasn't sure what to make of the conversation. It was clear that Grace was upset, and Regina didn't blame her for that. But there was an underlying tension. Regina wondered if it was Margot's last word directed at Grace—*youngish.*

She knew Grace was pragmatic about her age in a career that favoured the young. That was why she was attempting to get herself prepared for starting a new career. But it can't have been nice to have heard the pointed comment, especially from someone like Margot who was aiming to use it as a blunt weapon.

Regina regretted Grace being brought into the middle of the war between her and Margot. She just hoped that agreeing to Margot's terms would take Grace out of the line of fire. But this new and wholly unpredictable Margot wasn't someone Regina thought she could read.

❖

Arriving on set, Regina greeted Thomas and took her customary seat next to him and in front of the monitors. The models were walking around the new set in dressing gowns, chatting and sipping drinks from straws.

It felt like any other day running photo shoots for Amandine, but there was a cloud hanging over Regina. Where she'd usually smile at Grace and maybe even expect her to come over and greet her, that was firmly off the table. The only bright point in an otherwise disconcerting part of her working day had been firmly snuffed out by Margot.

"You've seen the call sheet?" Thomas asked.

Regina hadn't. She'd greeted Arjun and then entered her office and immediately remembered the evening before. It felt dramatic to say it was a return to the scene of the crime, but it had shaken her and thrown her off her normal morning schedule. Instead of preparing for the workday, she'd gone to the kitchen and found someone to make small talk with. Anything to shake her mood and the memories of the night before.

"No, I had a call which overran," she lied.

Thomas didn't seem to mind. He ran through the details of the call sheet, the line, the shots expected, and the plan of action. Regina corrected a couple of his assumptions. She might have known little about lingerie, but her ability to time manage was exceptional. A few changes to the order would easily save them fifteen minutes in equipment repositioning for the second half of the shoot.

It reminded her that she loved her job. Marketing was something that she was undeniably good at. She enjoyed the challenges as much as the wins. If Amandine had sold any other product, she would have considered staying, Margot be damned. Regina knew her value and ability.

"Get me a chair, Arjun."

Regina snapped her head around so quickly she was briefly worried about whiplash. Margot had entered the studio and was marching towards her, heels clacking hard against the concrete floor.

Arjun placed a chair next to Regina, where Margot was pointing, and sensibly backed away. Regina wished she could join him. Lurking in the shadows against the back wall sounded like a lovely place to be.

"Talk me through today," Margot demanded. She hadn't even looked at Regina since she'd sat down. Regina wondered if it was guilt following her behaviour from the day before, or if she literally couldn't be bothered to show Regina a scrap of decency until she finally cowed to Margot's authority.

In which case, she might be waiting a while.

Regina would do what was demanded of her, within reason. She'd agree to be shadowed, she'd agree to not see models off-shoot, and she'd cc Margot on every single email she sent. But there was a line. And she knew that deep down Margot knew it, too. One of the things Margot supposedly liked about her was her level-headed nature. And that very trait was what would stop Regina from getting caught up in Margot's web ever again.

She ran through the plan for the day, deliberately looking straight at Margot—or at least the side of her face—as she did. Let it be known that she would act like a sensible adult here even if Margot wouldn't.

Margot nodded. Her gaze was fixed on the models. Regina didn't look to see if it was Grace who was mainly under Margot's beady eye. She didn't want to be caught even glancing at the models after the previous evening.

"Let's get started," Margot said, cutting Regina's explanation of the schedule off mid-sentence.

Regina bit the inside of her cheek and sat back in her chair, looking down at her feet.

"Righto," Thomas said.

The shoot started, and within a minute, Margot had something to say. Regina gritted her teeth. Sitting silently, she watched as Margot started issuing direction. Make-up were called, Thomas was repositioned, and models were moved in and out of shot with sharp clicks of her fingers.

The resulting photographs would all be usable. And for that reason, Regina sat it out and allowed Margot her power play. Energy crackled from Margot as she stalked the space, barking instructions.

Regina reminded herself that it could only last for a short period of time. The shoot would soon be over. And, as unlikely as it felt, she'd soon be in a new job at another company. One day in the—hopefully—not too distant future, Amandine would be a blip on her career history. Something she laughed about as she shared battle stories with new colleagues about old bosses from hell.

One day.

CHAPTER NINETEEN

A week passed. A week of Margot glued to her side during every minute of the working day. A week of Regina never feeling so alone at work. While she met with other people, Margot was always there and monitoring her every word. The early days of feeling smug in her own small efforts to sabotage Margot had definitely worn off.

The only positive was that she'd become closer to Arjun. He'd not said anything specific, but he'd given off signals which indicated he also thought Margot was hanging on to reality by a thread. While it was nice to have the confirmation that she wasn't the only person seeing the complete mental collapse of a colleague, it made little difference.

She'd taken to leaving the office at five on the dot, pretending that she had a yoga class to get to. Her working hours were technically nine to five, but Regina had never worked those hours in her life. She'd always gotten in early and left late, never to show up her colleagues, try to earn a promotion, or simply to be seen, but because she liked her work.

That feeling had worn off, and now she dawdled to work in the morning, stopping in at various branches of the same popular chain of coffee shops to pick up her morning tea. While she wasn't quite brave enough to change up her drink order, or even try a different chain, she had made a pact with herself to at least try a new branch each morning. It gave her something to do and some new input when inside her mind she felt as though she was climbing invisible walls. Stuck at Amandine. Stuck under Margot's control.

She walked into the last branch of the familiar chain on her journey to work. It was quite near to the office but she'd never been inside. It looked like all the other stores. The baristas wore the same aprons, the design was familiar, but the only difference was the size of the space. This one was larger than the one the day before, but smaller than her favourite by St. James's Park.

She sighed to herself. Her life was so empty that she had started comparing coffee shops. The highlight of her day was seeing a new location and thinking *Yes, this is the same as the other locations.* It was like a weird hobby she had taken on in order to forget how depressed she was feeling. Not to mention how she was clinging on to something she could control in such a topsy-turvy world.

She placed her order and walked away from the mass of people to stand against the far wall. Her order required hot water being placed in a cup, but she knew that didn't mean that she would get her drink any quicker. She liked her favourite chain because they worked fairly and methodically.

While other patrons crowded the pickup area, frustrated that the next order wasn't there despite there always having been ten people in front of them, Regina stood out of the way. She wasn't one for people watching. People were far too irritating, especially in crowds. But she did enjoy people avoiding, a system that involved knowing what a group of people would do and doing her best to stay out of their combined madness.

She zoned in on a business type. He was checking his phone and sighing loudly as he looked around the crowded pickup bench. His body language said that he felt he was far too important to be waiting in a queue of people. The fact that he was waiting spoke volumes at his inability to work with others and thereby earn a promotion that would allow him to send an assistant to get his drink for him. Her thoughts turned to Arjun and the obvious fact that he was destined to be far more than an assistant. She'd started considering a coaching plan for him and was planning to make introductions between him and other teams. Career progression at Amandine would lead him right to Margot's door, and she liked him too much for that.

It was then that she realised she recognised the latest customer to enter the store. Her panic instinct kicked in before she had truly identified who it was, and it took her a moment to organise her thoughts and realise that she was face to face with Grace.

"Hi." She couldn't help but smile.

It disarmed a confused Grace, who was clearly wondering if they were able to communicate. "Hi. How are you?"

Regina didn't want to answer honestly. She was in a pretty bleak place and knew better than to bring the mood down by admitting as much.

"I'm okay. How are you doing? Did you sign up for that course?"

Grace came alive as she nodded. "I did. After I signed up for the newsletter, they sent me a code for money off the course if I signed up within five days. Which I suppose is why it's such a good marketing course."

Regina nodded. "Nothing like a time-sensitive offer to push a prospect to become a customer."

"Yep. I fell for it. I love a deal. A good sale gets me out of bed in the morning." She gestured towards the cashier. "Have you ordered?"

Regina nodded. "Yes, I'm just staying out of the scrum."

"Good thinking. I'll be back in a moment."

Regina watched as Grace greeted the cashier with a big smile and a seemingly genuine enquiry about their morning. She looked over the menu, eyes wide with excitement at all the products on offer and verbally wondering what to have.

Regina looked at menus but never dared move away from her usual order. She didn't know if she looked at the offerings to be polite, give the impression she was making a decision, or because there was a small part of her itching for something new.

A couple of minutes went by and Grace returned. "Have you tried the new porridge?"

Regina shook her head. Breakfast was always had at home, and it was often the same thing. But she wasn't about to tell Grace that.

"It sounds yummy."

"It does," Regina agreed.

"I'm waiting for their Christmas treats to come out. They do this adorable brownie that looks like a reindeer. I get it every year, and I go to Trafalgar Square to see the tree. It's a little tradition." Grace's eyes sparkled, and Regina could feel herself getting lost in them.

"I like the mince pie," Regina said. "Usually, a good mince pie needs to be served hot with custard, but the version they have here is pretty good, so I can forgive it being cold."

"Mince pies should be served cold with whipped cream." Grace said it matter-of-factly, but her grin suggested she was teasing.

Regina made a face of faux disgust. "No, no. Absolutely not."

Grace laughed. "Okay, what about Christmas pudding?"

"Well, my father always had it with ice cream. But his taste buds were cause for concern. I'd have Christmas pudding with whipped cream."

"I'll have to try that. I usually have it plain."

Regina shook her head. "Plain? That's illegal, I'm quite sure of it."

Whatever Grace said next disappeared in the rush of panic that caused Regina to hear nothing and see nothing save for Margot walking past the coffee shop. A moment later, Margot returned. She'd definitely spotted them and was now heading into the store to investigate for herself.

"Shit," Regina mumbled.

The smile left Grace's face as she turned to see what had caused Regina's good mood to vanish.

"Morning, Margot," Regina said cheerfully. "Looks like we've all stopped into the same place for our morning caffeine."

Margot looked from Grace to Regina with suspicion clear in her gaze.

"Well, I always come here," Grace said, a fake smile now plastered on her face. "It's you two who are the newcomers. As I was saying to Regina, I thoroughly recommend the oat latte they make here."

"She'll have tea—she always does," Margot said.

Grace shrugged. "Well, if she ever wants to mix it up. Anyway, I think I heard my name being called."

Grace left Regina's side without a goodbye and joined the scrum of people collecting drinks. Margot made her way to the cashier. Regina watched as Grace caught the attention of one of the baristas and spoke with him. A few moments later, she was handed a drink and quickly made her escape.

Regina's name was called, and she entered the crowd of people to grab her drink. She stood for a moment, wondering if she should try to escape Margot and catch up with Grace to offer yet another apology.

"This queue is ridiculous. Don't they know we're busy people," Margot said loudly to Regina. Loud enough so everyone else in the store could hear. Regina gripped her drink and stayed silent. She hoped that any normal person would see her body language and realise she was a hostage to the situation and not an active participant.

She was glad this wasn't her usual branch. If it had been, it would sadly no longer be.

CHAPTER TWENTY

Thomas looked at Regina. She shrugged.

It was silently assumed by all that Margot would attend the photo shoot. She was never scheduled to be there, but over the course of the last week she'd turned up at and ruled over every one of them.

"We'll struggle to finish if we don't start soon," Thomas pointed out.

Regina sighed. She looked at her watch. It was twenty-five minutes past the time they were scheduled to begin. She debated calling Margot but didn't want to speak to her after the encounter at the coffee shop that morning. Nor did she want to give Margot the opportunity to sneer that Regina couldn't cope without her.

"Let's start," Regina agreed.

"Great." Thomas leapt into action. His energy had been noticeably sapped by the micromanagement from Margot over the last week. He'd gone from excitedly bouncing around the set to lifelessly pointing the lens wherever Margot instructed and pressing the shutter button.

Arjun entered the studio and approached Regina. After ten minutes had passed, she'd sent him to look for Margot.

"Anything?" she whispered.

"Not in her office. But she's been in this morning. Nothing on her schedule," he said.

"Dare we hope she's forgotten about us?" Regina mused.

"Doubtful," he said.

"Well, thank you for trying."

Arjun nodded and discreetly headed towards the back of the room where his laptop was set up.

The screen in front of her snapped to life every time Thomas took a shot. Sometimes it held a single image for minutes while he issued instruction. But during bursts of shots, it flashed quickly and almost became a stop motion animation.

Regina tentatively looked at the screen. A host of images flashed into being. Her gaze was drawn to Grace, drawn to the beautiful smile. She was again struck by how unfair it was that they were being separated by Margot's unwarranted jealousy.

Bess's voice echoed in her head, encouraging her to tell Grace that she liked her. It was ridiculous to think that Grace could ever feel the same, but in the safe privacy of her own mind she allowed the notion to briefly run wild. To be greeted in the morning by that smile would be something special.

"Thomas! Can we pause there, please?" Margot's voice jolted Regina back to reality.

The fact she had said please was a cause for concern. Regina turned to look at her and was surprised to see a wide, genuine smile on Margot's face. Something was up, and Regina didn't like it one bit.

Thomas sagged in frustration and walked back from the set to where Regina sat. Margot approached, lowering her voice as she spoke to Thomas. "We're making a change. We'll need to start over for this scene, I'm sorry, darling."

Thomas frowned in confusion but raised a shoulder casually. "You're the boss."

"Thank you," Margot said, sickly sweet. "We made a late decision on Grace Holland, you see. The execs have looked at some of the shots, and they're in agreement that she's aged out for this collection."

Thomas looked surprised but said nothing.

Regina was appalled. "Margot—"

Margot silenced her with one glare. Her expression turned from one of pure joy to ice in a second. "The decision is made."

"We're too far in to be—"

"We'll work with what we have," Margot insisted. "Not our decision to argue with the execs."

Regina wanted to argue. She wanted to scream the building down. It was very much within their remit to argue with the executives. Not to mention that the executives had clearly been driven to the decision by Margot. No one at that level of seniority was looking over shoot photos of their own initiative. Margot had taken a suggestion to them.

"Grace?" Margot called to the set. "Can we have a chat, dear?"

Grace looked worried, and Regina wished she could give her some kind of warning for what was coming. Or better still, stop the whole thing. But she knew that Margot's mind was made up and the wheels had been put in motion.

Thomas headed off, wisely not wanting to be around when someone was fired.

Grace approached, pulling her robe tightly closed around her.

Margot made a face, which was presumably supposed to look like she was sad, but she couldn't quite manage it and a hint of joy was still seen gleaming in her eyes.

"I'm so sorry, but we're going to be parting company," Margot said.

"Oh." Grace looked shell-shocked.

"Yes, it's terribly sad, isn't it?" Margot continued.

"Is something wrong with the shots?" Grace asked. "I can—"

"Nothing like that," Margot said with faux reassurance. "It's actually a little difficult to say, but, well, the higher-ups have had a look at the portfolio, and they wonder if maybe you're not a good fit for this range. Or, really, for Amandine. I hate to be the one to say this but, you know, age-wise."

Grace's mouth dropped open slightly, and Regina thought she saw tears start to gather in her eyes. Regina wanted to reassure her and tell her that it was all down to Margot and no one else, but she knew nothing would help now. Margot wanted Grace gone, and that was that.

"I know, I know," Margot said. "It's so very sad, for all of us. We loved working with you but…well, you must have been expecting this at some point. We all lose our looks eventually."

"Margot," Regina snapped.

"Oh, I don't mean it like that, of course. You're still a very beautiful woman. It's just that we're not a good fit. I'm sure you'll find other jobs." Margot reached out and placed a hand on Grace's upper arm. "It would be professional of you to not make a scene and just slip out quietly."

Grace nodded and quickly turned away, not saying goodbye or even making eye contact with Regina before she vanished into the dressing room.

"I can't believe you did that," Regina said.

"Did what? I'm just the messenger, Regina," Margot insisted.

Regina didn't buy a word of it. Margot had seen them in the coffee shop that morning and had made a decision there and then to get Grace out of Amandine.

"Right, let's get this back on track, shall we?" Margot called out to the confused models who remained on the set. "Thomas, let's go back to the start."

Margot approached the set and started to position the models. She looked delighted, as if she had a winning lottery ticket in her pocket.

Arjun appeared beside Regina. "What just happened?"

"She's fired Grace."

Arjun raised an eyebrow. "Why?"

Regina turned to face him. "Because the higher-ups think she's too old."

Arjun's face said it all. In the second before he could compose himself, bafflement and disbelief flooded his expression. "Should I call her agent?"

"I imagine Margot's taken care of everything. And I imagine it brought her a tremendous amount of joy," Regina said.

❖

Grace unlocked her apartment door on the third attempt, her key missing the lock because of her shaky hand the first two times. She'd been holding back tears the entire way home. The desire to cry had been strong, and she promised herself that she could have a complete emotional collapse once she got home.

The moment she closed the door behind her, she leaned her back against the door and slid to the floor. Tears tore through her as she sobbed openly.

She'd lost jobs before but never in such a heartless way. Margot's firing technique was cold and personal, designed to hurt Grace as much as possible while pretending to be professional. The callous grin would be burned into Grace's memory for some time to come.

The public firing was uncalled for and terribly embarrassing. While her colleagues hadn't necessarily heard Margot's words, they knew what had happened.

Worst of all, Regina had been right there. She'd tried to stop Margot, but even Grace knew it was a pointless endeavour. Margot had made up her mind, her obvious lust for Regina blinding her. Being fired was terrible—being fired by your crush's ex was even worse.

As horrible as it was to lose a job, and frightening to think that she might really be aging out of her profession, the thought of never seeing Regina again lay heavily on her chest. There was a very real possibility that Grace seeing Regina in the future could have serious repercussions for Regina if Margot was ever to find out.

As much as it hurt, she knew she needed to stay away from Regina to protect her from Margot's wrath.

Chapter Twenty-one

Regina looked at her online calendar and was surprised to note that it had been a week since Margot had callously fired Grace. A week where Regina had emotionlessly done her job and interacted with Margot as little as she could manage. A week where she had spent every evening looking for another job and checking in with Bess for distraction.

Days were passing quickly, not because she was enjoying her job or had come to some sort of peace with her situation, but because she had turned off entirely. Bess implored her to quit, but Regina wouldn't do it. At this point it would be letting Margot win her twisted little game.

Margot had worked to isolate Regina in the hope that it would drive them together. But Regina was determined to prove that it would only serve to drive them apart. She'd given up wondering what was going on with Margot. Any hint of concern had evaporated when she'd fired Grace in the way she did.

Regina blew out a sigh and looked at her phone. She longed to reach out to Grace again, but she knew she should respect Grace's obvious request for space.

It was lunchtime on the day Grace had walked out of Amandine for the last time when Regina had finally found time to make the phone call. Grace hadn't answered. Regina had sent a text message, apologising for Margot and saying how sorry she was to have clearly been the reason for Grace having to leave.

Grace had replied to the text not long after, a clear indication that she hadn't wanted to talk and had been screening her calls. She'd told Regina it wasn't her fault and that it was probably for the best. She finished the short message by saying that she wished her well, which Regina considered to be extraordinarily kind considering the situation. She didn't know if she'd be so understanding just three hours after being fired in such a manner.

Regina's two following texts had never received a reply. One was sent straight away, the second three days later. Both had been read.

Arjun knocked on the open office door.

Regina pushed her phone to one side and smiled to welcome him into the room.

He placed some magazines down on the desk. "These are the back copies you requested. I've put a sheet of paper in where the ads are and noted down the media buyer and the costs."

It was far above and beyond what he needed to do.

"You didn't need to do that," she told him. "But I do appreciate it."

He picked out one of the magazines and placed it on the top of the pile. "This is the article I mentioned yesterday, about the gender-free line at Apocalypse."

She picked up the magazine and leafed through to the page indicated. "As I said yesterday, I don't disagree with you. I would love to see Amandine go in this direction, not just for publicity but because it's the right thing to do. But I'm not knowledgeable enough to be able to pitch this. You are, though." She looked up at him.

He flushed. "Me?"

"You. It's your idea."

"Who's going to listen to me?"

"You're a smart, articulate person with a lot of industry knowledge and an idea supported by market trends as well as ROI projections. Everyone should listen to you." Regina tapped the article. "I see they went with genderless rather than gender-free?"

"Yes, there's a split in the industry about which way to go. It's pretty evenly split."

"That won't last," Regina said. "They'll come down on gender-free. Less indicates you are lacking, missing something. Free, well, you're free. It has far better connotations. It's like the difference between being childless and child-free—someone who chooses to not have children wouldn't want to consider themselves less. Words matter. Especially in these areas."

"That's why you should present this," he insisted. "I didn't know that."

"And now you do, adding to your impressive amount of knowledge in this area. Honestly, Arjun, if I presented this, I would either have no idea what I was talking about or I'd simply be presenting your work. No, I'll set up a time for you to speak with Margot."

"Margot?" His eyebrows rose. Her name was not willingly spoken of in Regina's office, and never in a positive light.

"She's in charge of our team. She'd be the natural person to present to." Regina knew for sure that Margot would be delighted to receive a good idea from Arjun. Any groundbreaking strategies developed by her team would be accredited to Margot in some way.

"If you're sure?"

"I'm sure. Pull together a presentation, I'll review it for you, and then you can present to Margot. If she thinks the idea has merit, she'll take it forward."

"But she—"

"Is the boss," Regina said. "If you want to get ahead at Amandine, then you'll need to take personality differences out of it."

Arjun nodded sharply. "Agreed. Yes, I'll put my thoughts into a presentation. Thank you."

He hurried out of the office, presumably ready to start drafting the presentation immediately. Her phone pinged and she snatched it up in the hope that it was Grace. Her heart skipped a beat when she saw it was an email from a recruitment consultant.

She scanned the email and was quickly flooded with disappointment. She'd sent her CV for a role that had looked quite promising a couple of days earlier. She'd felt for sure that she would be a good candidate for the role, but apparently her experience wasn't a good enough match and she wasn't even being called in for an interview.

She tossed her phone back onto the desk and blew out a breath. She'd forgotten about this part of the process. It wasn't just waiting for jobs to be advertised—it was getting in the door and to the interview stage. She made a mental note to do some research to make sure her CV was the best it could be. It had been a while since she'd needed to refresh it.

Arjun returned with a large, flat, rectangular package wrapped in brown paper.

"I completely forgot that I asked for this to be sent up," he said. "It's so empty in here—I thought you could do with some artwork. There were some spare pieces left over when they were redoing the hallway on the top floor. I thought we could brighten up the space."

"This space?" Regina didn't particularly want her space to be brightened up. She liked it to feel temporary. Decorating made it feel as though she might be staying.

He started ripping the brown paper but stopped dead. "Maybe this wasn't the best idea." He looked at her with wide, worried eyes.

Regina stood up and walked around the desk. "Only one way to find out." She ripped at the paper and tossed it to the floor.

The framed image was none other than Grace Holland wearing a strapless evening dress in navy blue, straight from the eveningwear line. She'd been Photoshopped onto a skyscraper balcony with her hair flowing as if caught by the wind. It was a different vibe to the lingerie line. This Grace was smiling and carefree, and had a twinkle in her eye.

"Should I, um, take it away again?" Arjun asked softly.

Regina wanted to keep it but knew that Margot would lose her mind if there was a framed print of Grace in her office. Even Arjun had caught on to Margot's personal vendetta against Grace.

"Yes, I think you better."

"I'm sorry, I should have checked what the leftover pictures were. I didn't think." He picked up the frame and started to leave. "We don't want to send Margot into a fit."

"No, we don't," Regina agreed. She thought for a moment. "Arjun, wait. Let's put it on the wall outside my office."

Arjun frowned. "Are you sure?"

"Absolutely. It's not in my office. If Margot wants it taken down, then she'll have to make a scene in the main office where everyone will see her."

Arjun smiled. "That's a good point. Sure. I'll find a place for it."

"If she asks, you have no idea who put it up. Let's keep this our little secret."

He nodded and headed off with the picture to find it a new home.

Regina smiled to herself. Margot would be furious to see Grace's effortless beauty hanging just outside Regina's office. While she might have control over the marketing department walls, and even Regina's office, she didn't have a say in what hung on the main office walls. Models from decades ago were still proudly displayed in the foyer, and so there was no real argument for Grace not to be admired by all.

But of course, mainly by Regina.

CHAPTER TWENTY-TWO

Regina had walked alone through London all her adult life. While she was always cautious, she rarely felt as if she was in any real danger. Like anyone else, she took the appropriate precaution of walking in well-lit, populated areas. Most importantly, she was mindful of her surroundings and paid close attention to other people on the streets.

Which was how she knew that she was being followed. It had been a suspicion at first. Just a feeling that danced around her paranoia. But soon enough it had become obvious, through the sound of the same footsteps which slowed when Regina had slowed. Whoever was following her was seemingly unwilling to pass her. Shadows cast by streetlights also confirmed that the same person walked in her footsteps block after block.

She was ten minutes from home. Close but not close enough. Traffic had thinned out as she'd had to walk away from the main road and into the residential side streets near where she lived.

Fear gripped her but soon gave way to anger, anger that someone was making her feel unsafe when she was walking home. Anger that people had to go through this on a daily basis. Anger overall at life and how much pressure she felt.

She'd never been one to carry something that could be used as a weapon, all too aware that someone could easily overpower her and take control of it. While she liked to think she could cover her attacker with a mist of pepper spray, she knew the reality was that she'd end up with a face full of the nasty chemical herself.

But Bess had insisted she carry a whistle. Sweet, innocent Bess, born in years gone by, who thought that people would come running towards the sound of danger and help rescue them. Regina had always thought it unlikely. But now, reaching for her whistle, buried in the very depth of her bag just next to the lip balm she had lost over six months ago, she hoped she was wrong.

She sucked in a deep breath and prepared herself to confront her stalker. She spun around and held up her whistle.

"Stop or I'll raise the alarm!"

The stalker stopped dead in their tracks. The two of them stood in between streetlights, and all Regina could make out was a figure wrapped in many layers of winterwear to keep out the late autumn winds. The figure raised their hands.

"Regina, it's me," a familiar voice called out.

It took her a couple of seconds to put the pieces together and realise that this stalker wasn't a threat at all.

"Grace?"

Grace stepped forward. "I'm so sorry. I didn't think you'd noticed me, so I just kept back. I shouldn't have followed you like that."

Regina let out a sigh of relief. "Oh, thank goodness it's you. You scared me."

"I know. I'm so sorry." Grace looked at the whistle. "Wow. Cute."

Regina looked at the pink plastic whistle with a hideous amount of glitter embedded into it. "Thank you. My aunt bought it. I believe these ladies are Disney Princesses?"

Grace peered at the peeling sticker. "Yep. They are."

Regina smiled. Grace could defuse her so quickly and easily. She'd missed her presence. Which led to an obvious question. "Why were you following me?"

"I'm not. I'm walking home."

"Oh." Regina felt silly for her assumption that someone like Grace would have any interest in following her. "I didn't know you lived around here."

"My new apartment is nearby. I'm so sorry. I spotted that it was you, and I was going to cross the road or do something, but I didn't want you to see me."

"Why not?"

Grace looked at her as if she were stupid. "In case Margot sees us together and sends one of us to the gallows."

"Ah. Yes, well, she doesn't get a say in whether or not we walk together on a public street. Besides, she lives out of the city—she'd never be around here." Regina gestured to the path ahead. "Shall we?"

Grace took hold of Regina's arm and squeezed it as they walked. "I'm sorry I didn't reply to your messages. I've been sulking."

"You have every right to sulk," Regina said. "But maybe you could sulk to me rather than away from me? I've missed you."

Regina tried not to overthink how nice it felt to have Grace holding on to her arm as they walked. It was just a kind gesture from a sweet person. She was sure Grace did the same with all her friends.

"I've missed you, too. I didn't want to cause any more trouble for you."

"You didn't cause the trouble—I did."

"No, Margot did."

"Yes, but it wouldn't have happened if it wasn't for me. We share the blame."

Grace chuckled. "I don't understand why you're always willing to take the blame for Margot's behaviour."

"I suppose it's because I know that she won't apologise."

"Doesn't mean that you should on her behalf."

"I suppose you're right. I just feel so terribly bad about what happened. I hope you know that she went to the execs herself with her ridiculous concerns. No one had a question about your age or how you look. She wanted to sow the seeds to get rid of you. Because she's jealous of you."

"I'm not giving her another thought," Grace insisted, in a way that didn't quite sound convincing. "How are you, anyway? Are you managing? Any new jobs on the horizon?"

Regina laughed bitterly. "Nothing worth mentioning. And

we're getting closer to Christmas, and that generally means a hiring freeze until the new year. Which means I'll be spending at least a couple more months at Amandine."

The thought was depressing, but she knew she had to think realistically or she ran the risk of becoming far more depressed than she already was. She needed to keep her spirits up, and being realistic rather than optimistic would help.

"I'm sorry to hear that." Grace let go of Regina's arm and walked ahead to push the traffic light button. She immediately felt the chill at the loss. She hoped that Grace would come back and cuddle up to her again and was disappointed when she didn't.

"How are things with you? Enjoying the new place?"

The lights changed and they walked across the road. "I'm loving it. It's smaller than where I was, so it's easier to clean and far cosier. I need to change some furniture and think about decorating, but I think it's going to be a great home. Most of all…no noisy neighbours. Yet."

"Yet," Regina agreed. "They may just be on holiday."

Grace laughed. "Don't!"

"Maybe it's another rock star who is touring. I mean, have you actually seen all your neighbours yet? You used to live next door to the guitarist—maybe you're next door to the drummer now?"

"Uch! No!" Grace smiled. "No. I'll just have to move in with you if that happens."

Regina laughed, happy for the dim lighting and the fact they were walking side by side and knowing that her blush was safe. "Me? Why me?"

"Because you just jinxed it."

"Oh, so if it happens, it will only be because I breathed life into it as a concept?"

"Of course. I'll blame you one hundred percent. I'll turn up at your door with a suitcase. And my coffee maker. I can't live without my coffee maker."

"I've never known you to drink coffee."

"I have a big bucket of it every morning and a special decaffeinated blend of an evening. I'm very serious about my coffee," Grace said. "In fact, I found a really amazing place with tons of great reviews just around the corner from my new place. I need to try it out."

"There's a place near me that had influencers falling over themselves to get this doughnut-croissant-muffin concoction they created. I hear they do incredibly good coffee."

Grace stopped walking. Regina stopped and looked at her in confusion.

"You don't mean Mister Beans?" Grace asked.

"Yes, that's the place." Regina felt the penny drop. "Wait, where do you live now?"

"Archibald Street."

Regina laughed. "That is literally around the corner from me."

Grace beamed. "Really? Cool! So much easier to get to when that drummer comes home from holiday."

They chuckled and continued walking. Regina felt strangely happier to know that Grace lived so close by, even though it technically meant nothing changed between them.

"Want to go to Mister Beans sometime?" Grace said. "I bet they do plain tea. And then I can see what all the fuss is about."

Regina couldn't think of anything she'd like more. In fact, the thought of it caused a moment of brain fog, which meant she remained silent for a beat too long.

"Unless you think Margot may—"

"Fuck Margot," Regina said, aware it was the first time she'd ever used such language around Grace.

Grace snorted a laugh.

"Sorry. I'd love to," Regina said. "When?"

"Um. I'm free tomorrow," Grace suggested. "Unless that's too soon?"

"Tomorrow sounds perfect." Regina knew she'd be counting down the minutes.

Regina was aware that she had set a slower pace than she would normally walk, knowing that their time together was coming to an end as her road approached. They talked about the area and the local shops before Regina had to say goodbye.

"This is me." She gestured to the road.

"Oh. Okay. Thanks for walking with me and not blowing your Disney whistle in my face."

Regina rolled her eyes playfully at the dig.

"Mister Beans at…six?" Grace suggested.

"That works for me."

They hesitated a moment, each clearly not sure how to say goodbye. Eventually, Regina took a step away and raised her hand in a half wave. "Goodnight."

"'Night."

Regina watched for a beat as Grace turned and walked away. She fought the urge to catch up to her and claim she remembered an errand she had to run that would allow them a few more precious minutes together. She shook her head and made her way home.

CHAPTER TWENTY-THREE

Margot entered Regina's office without knocking and threw a stack of paperwork down onto the desk. Regina looked up from her laptop and waited for an explanation.

"This is all the market share information. It was never digitized. You might want to get Arjun to do that," Margot said.

Margot delivering something by hand had become an unwelcome feature of Regina's week. It hadn't escaped Regina's notice that Margot appeared to enjoy delivering items which she hoped would provoke a response. A ridiculous number of back copies of magazines, undigitized research, printed mock-ups with obvious errors on them, all came to Regina by Margot's hand. And every time, Margot watched over Regina, waiting for a response. And Regina declined to give her what she wanted.

Sometimes it was harder than others to keep a neutral expression. There had been days when Margot had done her best to break down Regina's resolve throughout the day like a death by a thousand cuts before hand-delivering the final nail in the coffin. Today had been one of those days.

Margot had commented on Regina's good mood that morning and had subsequently spent more time than usual popping into Regina's office to discuss things that supposedly popped into her mind. Margot was clearly curious about the smile that Regina knew lingered on her face and attempted to break through her icy exterior.

"Okay, thank you," Regina said.

Margot wasn't going to break her spirit today. And Regina wasn't going to try to antagonise her either. It was a day for a truce. The only thing that would irritate Regina was the slow passing of time before she could leave the office and get to the coffee shop and see Grace again.

She'd spent the previous evening lost in a daydream, thanking her lucky stars that she did turn around to confront whoever had been following her. She could quite easily have sped up her walk home and never turned around. Never had felt Grace hold her arm as they walked.

"What's going on with you?" Margot asked, obviously unable to take not knowing any longer.

"What do you mean?" Regina picked up the papers and started to leaf through them. They were nonsense, something mentioned in passing that had a sudden relevance now that Margot wanted a reason to see her.

"You're…happy."

"Heaven forbid."

"Happier than usual," Margot continued. "Is there something I should know about?"

"My aunt has a new man in her life. She's happy, and that makes me happy," Regina said. It was technically true, and it was hopefully enough to shake Margot off the trail.

She'd only met Bess a couple of times, by choice. Any time Regina made plans for them to both go and see Bess, Margot had a sudden conflict or illness or simply pouted like a child being made to go to school. In the end, Regina had visited alone, which had turned out to be better for everyone involved.

But Margot was very aware of how important Bess was to Regina, and therefore the lie about her sudden good mood would hopefully be accepted at face value.

Margot looked at her for a few seconds and then winced. "At her age?"

"Yes, at her age. I don't suppose love has an expiry date."

"Sounds disgusting. Do they…" Margot shook her head. "No. I don't want to know."

"Good, because I hadn't asked, and even if I had I wouldn't tell you."

Margot's face of displeasure grew in intensity. "I have a mental picture stuck in my head now."

"Well, you did ask." Regina tapped the papers. "Thank you for these. I'll review them and see if they are worth getting Arjun to digitize."

Margot nodded and walked out, seemingly eager to leave.

❖

Regina nervously arrived at the coffee shop five minutes early. She had no idea where the nerves had suddenly come from. Nearly twenty-four hours' worth of eagerness had vanished as she walked home—peeking over her shoulder in case Grace was walking behind her.

If she allowed herself to be honest, she'd admit that the nerves were because of her growing less than platonic feelings towards Grace. Every time she caught her thoughts straying away from friendship, she mentally shook herself out of it. Grace was nothing more than a friend. It would be wrong of Regina to misinterpret Grace's expressively friendly nature as anything more.

Not that Regina had that sort of iron control over her feelings. She didn't really have any close friends, and so to be touched, even through the thick layers of her coat, was something she rarely experienced. It was natural that her emotions would run riot.

The important thing was for Regina to keep that to herself. While the uncomfortable power dynamic of technically being Grace's boss was out of the way, that didn't mean she wanted to ruin the friendship they had.

She entered the coffee shop and looked around the familiar space. She'd visited a couple of times when she'd moved in, but not so much lately. For Regina, coffee shops were for when she was away from home and wanted a beverage to take to the office, on a journey, or into a meeting. When she was so close to home, she'd much rather make it herself.

It occurred to her then that proved that she didn't socialise often. Looking around the space, she saw people from all walks of life catching up with one another. She felt a little out of place as she found an empty table to wait for Grace.

She wondered if it had really been so long since she'd socialised with a friend that she now felt out of place doing so. The answer was a resounding yes. Her life had been work for so long.

She was torn from her thoughts by Grace entering the shop.

"This is cute," she announced, loud enough for anyone listening to hear. Regina smiled at the casual confidence that Grace exuded. Regina would never walk into a space and announce her thoughts in the way Grace had done. But it seemed so normal and natural for Grace to do so. Even the barista was smiling at Grace's honest reaction.

Grace placed her bag on the floor and wrestled herself out of her multiple winter layers, placing them on a nearby coat stand that Regina hadn't even seen. It was then she realised she was still wearing her own coat and looked like someone waiting for a train rather than someone preparing to sit and chat with a friend. She shrugged her coat off and hung it on the back of the chair.

Grace was still looking around the shop. "I love this place. I bet you come here all the time."

"Rarely," Regina admitted. "I haven't had much time."

"Shame." Grace reached into her bag and plucked up her purse. She walked over to the counter. "What do you want? My treat."

Regina hesitated to leave all her belongings on the table but followed Grace's lead.

Grace looked up at the extensive menu with awe.

"I'll obviously have my usual, but you don't need to buy it for me," Regina said.

"I know, but I will," Grace said. She looked at the barista. "Hi, how are you?"

The barista smiled. "I'm great. How's your day been?"

"Cold!" Grace shivered a little. "Nice and warm in here, though. Let's see, can I have the almond latte? And some kind of little biscuity thing. What's good?"

The barista pointed out a couple of speciality snacks. Grace peered through the glass and bit her lip.

"Regina, you're going to have to help me. Let's get both of them and share, yes?"

"Yes, sure," Regina said, feeling a little discombobulated. Her interactions with cafe staff were never so lively. She placed her order—politely, of course—and moved on. Grace focused her full attention on the staff member in such a genuine manner that Regina couldn't help but be charmed by her further.

After Grace ordered Regina's tea and paid, the barista said they'd bring everything over to them.

"Love this place," Grace said as they sat down.

"Yes, it is…cute." Regina felt the word sounded out of place coming from her own mouth. "How are you? Other than cold?"

"Cold," Grace emphasised. "I had a water shoot today. Who does that in winter?"

Regina blinked. "You've been in water?"

"Yes, a designer decided to get in on the swimwear act. Clearly the whole thing is delayed if we're shooting in October. It was freezing in the pool, and of course he wanted underwater swimming shots."

"Surely they heat the water?" Regina couldn't imagine being submerged in cold water, in swimwear, and trying to look glamourous at the same time.

"A little. They can't do too much, or you'll see the steam in the cold air." Grace rolled her eyes. "There were three of us—we huddled for warmth between set-ups. I hit the sauna at the gym afterwards."

Regina swallowed and tried to push the imagery away. "Are you back there tomorrow?"

"No. We got everything we needed today. Water shoots are expensive, and this is a newish designer. Probably broke his marketing budget for one day's worth of shooting. I usually say no to these but…"

Grace broke eye contact and Regina realised she'd said more than she'd intended.

"But?" Regina asked.

"But it was a favour to a friend, so I couldn't say no," Grace said. Regina was fairly sure it was a lie, but she couldn't fathom what context she'd missed. As she debated whether or not to probe, their drinks and food arrived.

"Thank you so much, this looks amazing," Grace said.

"No problem. Hey, feel free to say no, but could I have your autograph? My brother is a big fan of yours." The barista held out an order pad and a pen, a hopeful look on their face.

"Sure." Grace took the pen and paper. "What name?"

Regina tried to keep the surprise off her face. She knew Grace was a relatively well-known model, but she'd never expected her to be signing autographs. She supposed it made sense—people would clearly recognise her, and anyone with an interest in fashion would surely know who she was.

The way Grace casually interacted with the barista and happily signed an autograph led Regina to believe this was a fairly regular occurrence.

Once they were alone again, Regina asked, "Does that happen often?"

Grace shrugged. "A bit, I guess. Some days I seem to fly under the radar, and others, several people might approach me. It's more selfies than autographs these days."

"I can't imagine what that must be like," Regina admitted.

"You get used to it. I'm lucky that it built up over time. I wasn't just suddenly famous one day. I think it would be a huge culture shock if it was out of the blue like that." Grace gestured to the two biscuits on the plate. "Which would you like to try first?"

Regina looked at the Christmas tree shape with vivid green icing and jelly sweets for baubles and then at the chocolate covered animal shape.

"I'll try this dog," she said.

"It's a reindeer," Grace said.

"No." Regina lifted it off the plate. "They want us to think it's a reindeer, but look at it."

Grace chuckled. "Don't be mean."

"Santa is not having his sleigh pulled by a fleet of these," Regina said. She broke it in two and took a bite. She moaned in delight at the mint chocolate flavouring hitting her palate. "Good, though."

Grace held out her hand and Regina handed her the other half of the biscuit. Grace took a bite and nodded as she chewed. "So good."

They ate and drank and told each other about their day. They were so involved in their conversation that it was only when the staff brought out a vacuum cleaner that they realised it was approaching closing time and they'd been talking for nearly two hours.

"We better get out of their hair," Grace said. She grabbed some money from her purse and put it in the glass jar by the till. "Thank you! Have a great night."

They put on their coats and headed outside. Regina wasn't ready for the night to be over, but she was also aware that it was late, and she couldn't monopolise any more of Grace's time.

"I didn't get to hear about your trip to Vienna," Grace said with a pout.

"We'll have to do this again sometime," Regina hinted.

"Definitely."

Regina couldn't help but smile at the confirmation Grace had also enjoyed their time together and, crucially, wanted to do it again. She started to walk home, Grace walking beside her.

"I'm starving," Grace said.

"Same. Biscuits for dinner isn't a good idea."

Grace got her mobile phone out of her pocket. "There's an Italian on this road that has good reviews."

"Is it Sergio's?"

"That's the one."

"I've been there a couple of times. They do very good pizza. Apparently authentic."

"Oh yes, pizza sounds great," Grace said. "Do you think they'll have a table available for us?"

Regina hesitated a second while she switched gears. She'd been prepared to go home and take some sub-par ready meal out of the freezer to eat alone.

"Actually, it's a weeknight—I'm sure it will be fine," Grace said.

"Yes, I'm sure it will," Regina said, hoping she sounded confident and not in shock at the sudden change of plans.

Grace pocketed her phone. "Great. Remind me to tell you about when I had supposedly authentic pizza in Italy only to find out later it was made by a Russian guy who all the locals hated."

"Sounds like you told me the highlights," Regina joked.

"Oh no, I haven't told you about the drugs raid happening in the back and the Vespa chase through the streets. It was quite the night."

Regina laughed. "It sounds it. Let's hope Sergio's is a little more sedate."

Chapter Twenty-four

A rjun looked concerned.

"I sent them to you an hour ago," he said.

Regina frowned. "Did you?"

"Yes, you approved them and sent them back." His brow knitted.

Regina looked from her assistant standing in the doorway to her laptop and checked her sent folder. Sure enough, she had seen the documents, reviewed them, and approved them, just a couple of hours ago.

"Oh yes." There wasn't much more she could say. She'd been off all day, and Arjun had definitely noticed. He'd hovered over her like a mother hen, offering to get her drinks from the kitchen and generally being overly attentive.

Her mind had been elsewhere since she arrived that morning, and she couldn't recall much of the day's work. Her distraction could be easily traced back to the night before with Grace.

They'd stayed until Sergio's closed, the second establishment forced to gently evict them in one evening. She'd walked Grace home where they said a friendly goodnight and both expressed an interest to meet up again soon. The second Regina walked away, she regretted not arranging a specific date. She'd been so eager to hide her romantic interest that she later worried she'd come off a little too aloof.

She'd gotten precious little sleep that evening as she replayed the night and kicked herself for not making firm plans with Grace for another time. The lack of sleep and swirling thoughts had followed her to the office and led to a very distracted day.

"I'm not feeling so well," she said. "I think I'm going to leave early and see if I can nip whatever this is in the bud."

"Sounds like a good idea. Do you want me to call you a taxi?" Arjun offered.

"No. Thank you, I'm sure I'll be fine. Call me if anything comes up, though."

❖

Instead of going home, Regina headed to Calm Acres to talk to the one person she knew she could speak with about what was on her mind. She'd called ahead from the train to say she was on her way. Bess must have detected the turmoil in her tone and said to come to her apartment where she'd have the kettle ready.

Some people thought it was cliché, but Regina and Bess had always proved the perception that British people dealt with emotional upset by putting on the kettle and making copious cups of tea. Tea didn't solve problems, but it made it easier to talk about them.

When she arrived, the door was partially open, and she could hear the sound of the radio coming from inside. She entered and called out a greeting before closing the door and hanging her coat in the hallway. She kicked off her boots and put them on the shoe rack.

In the kitchen, Bess was making tea and had a plate of biscuits ready. They shared a short, silent hug in greeting before sitting in the living room, Regina on the sofa and Bess in her armchair.

"Whenever you're ready, poppet," Bess said, sipping her tea.

Regina took a big gulp of tea. She licked her lips and then sat back on the sofa, grabbing a pillow and hugging it to her chest.

"I've fallen in love," she said softly.

"With the model?"

"Yes."

Bess didn't say anything. Regina knew unrest was coming off

her in waves, and Bess was allowing her the space she needed. They sat in silence for a couple more minutes before Regina elaborated.

"We met up last night. We went to a coffee shop to catch up. It was…wonderful," she explained. "We talked for so long they were closing up around us. We only actually noticed that everyone else had left and half the lights had been switched off when they brought the vacuum cleaner out."

Bess smiled and nodded for her to go on.

"I thought that was it and we'd go our separate ways. But we ended up sharing a pizza in a restaurant nearby. We had a couple of glasses of wine each, and before I knew it, they were closing for the evening, too." Regina squeezed the cushion tighter to herself. "She's so easy to talk to, Bess. We just have so much fun when we're together. She's like this burst of sunlight. I can't help but be happy when I see her."

"But?" Bess prompted.

"But we're just friends. I don't want to ruin that friendship, but I can't ignore how I feel either. It was a crush, but it's more than that now. I feel so strongly for her that I can't focus on anything else. I showered and used conditioner twice instead of any shampoo this morning. I forgot to put the dishwasher on and wondered why all the dishes were still dirty, but only after I'd unloaded half of them. I'm completely distracted by thoughts of her."

"You don't want to hear this," Bess said, "but maybe you need to tell her."

"No." Regina shook her head. "No, I can't do that. We have a perfectly lovely friendship. I don't want to ruin that."

"Maybe she feels the same way?"

Regina laughed. "Of course she doesn't. She's a young, attractive model. When we were in the coffee shop, someone asked for her autograph. Her autograph! We live in different worlds."

"But you seem to have a nice time when you're together."

"We do. But not like that."

They sat in silence for a while, each allowing the conversation to lull while they spent time with their thoughts.

"Maybe it's because I've found Leonard," Bess started. "But I think you should maybe think about saying something. If you fit together as well as you say, maybe she feels the same way."

Regina scoffed at the absurd thought.

"Can you turn off your feelings?" Bess asked.

Regina didn't need to consider the question. She shook her head. She was too far gone to be able to turn back time. Grace was in her every thought and every dream. No matter the short amount of time, it was love. She knew it. And love wasn't something that could be switched on and off. Once love existed, it took great heartbreak for it to vanish again.

"Then maybe you need to tell her," Bess said. "Because it might be too painful for you not to. If you love her, and you know that won't go away, then what kind of friendship is that?"

"I…don't want to hurt her. But I don't want to lose her either."

"You're so sure you'll lose her, why?" Bess asked.

Regina shook her head. "We're completely different people. She'd never be interested in someone like me. We're friends, nothing more."

"I think you have a bit of a warped view of yourself," Bess said. "You're a catch, Regina. You're very smart, kind, attractive. Anyone would be lucky to have you."

"You're my aunt—you're legally obligated to think that," Regina reminded her.

"No, if you were a miserable old sow, I'd tell you. Don't you worry about that." Bess grinned and they shared a small laugh. "You're risk averse, poppet," Bess continued. "Always have been. Since your parents left us."

Regina wanted to argue, but she knew it was true. She'd walked the safer path every day since she'd lost her parents. A cold chill crept up her spine whenever she considered doing something even mildly risky. Dull was what Margot had called her. As wrong as Margot was about most things, in that she was accurate.

"Is it so wrong to want to save a friendship?" Regina asked.

"You've already lost it, my love," Bess said. "Your feelings have changed. Not your fault, but they have. You can't go back to the way it was, you said that yourself. All you can do now is see if she feels the same way."

"I can ignore these feelings," Regina said.

Bess stared at her long and hard. "You don't believe that."

Regina ducked her head. It was true, she didn't believe it. She'd spent hours completely obsessed with the thought of Grace, and that wasn't going to change. The more time that went by, the more deeply she would fall. It was the way her heart worked.

"You didn't come here for advice," Bess said. "You came here because you wish you didn't feel the way you do and you want to unburden yourself. You know in your heart that your friendship with this Grace is over, and you have a difficult decision to make. Do you take the plunge and ask her out, or do you wait for the friendship to fizzle out?"

She was right. They both knew it.

"Now, how about some *Frost*?" Bess said, leaning forward and picking up the remote control.

Regina nodded. The TV show was irrelevant. She just wanted the comfort of being around her family, the only woman in the world who had been there for her entire life and knew Regina better than she knew herself. The familiar sights, sounds, and smells of sitting on a comfortable sofa, watching a TV show they could both recite by heart, and sipping the best tea she'd ever drink.

They'd watched three episodes by the time Regina looked at her watch and decided it was time to make her way home. Of course, Bess didn't want that. She followed Regina to the hallway and pouted as she put on her coat and boots.

"Stay," she insisted. "Leonard is coming over for dinner tonight with his grandson. There's obviously room for you, too."

"I don't want to intrude," Regina said.

"You're my north star, Regina," Bess said firmly. "Nothing and no one will ever change that, and you're never going to be intruding."

"Thank you, I appreciate hearing that," Regina confessed. "I suppose I mean I don't feel much like being in company right now."

"Well, you know my door is always open."

Regina hugged her close. "I know. Thank you for this afternoon. I needed this."

As they parted there was a knock on the door, six distinct raps in a jaunty tune.

"Leonard?" Regina asked knowingly.

Bess was already smiling. "Yes. He is a funny one."

Regina opened the door. If Leonard was surprised to see her, he didn't show it.

"Regina! Are you joining us?"

"I'm afraid not, just on my way home," she said.

Leonard looked at Bess. "What can we do to convince her to stay?"

Bess chuckled. "Nothing. She's as stubborn as I am."

A younger man in his thirties stepped forward. He pushed the hood of his hoodie down and held out his hand, "I'm Nick. The grandson."

Regina shook his hand. "Regina. The niece."

Nick smiled. "Sure you don't want to join us? We're watching *Frost*."

"Sounds lovely but I have plans," Regina lied smoothly. "Do send my regards to the inspector, though."

"Well, if you're busy tonight, then we'll have to get something booked in," Leonard said. "What are you doing on Saturday?"

Regina hesitated a moment, no immediate response ready to go.

"Looks like you're free, excellent." Leonard clapped his hands together. "I'm making my famous chicken pie."

"It's annoyingly really good, and he won't let anyone forget it," Nick added.

"It is pretty good," Bess added. "Do come and join us."

Regina was too tired to come up with an excuse, and so she nodded and found a burst of energy to feign enthusiasm. "Sounds like I must try this chicken pie, that sounds lovely. Thank you."

Leonard's eyes twinkled with excitement, and Regina saw exactly what Bess liked in the man. He lit up the room with his zest and joy. A little like someone else she knew. She pushed thoughts of Grace to the back of her mind. She still hadn't decided what to do about that situation and relished a few more days of ignoring the conundrum.

She said goodnight to the three, smiling to herself at Nick's apparent eagerness to get started on the Frostathon.

"I'm all for watching in order," she heard him say to Bess as she finished putting her gloves on. "But you have to appreciate the magnificence of series ten."

Bess rolled her eyes playfully. "But you have to build up the character arc, so you know why he acts the way he does. Isn't that right, Regina?"

"I'm sorry, I didn't quite catch any of that," she lied playfully. "Enjoy your evening, all."

On the way home, she held her phone in her hand and pondered whether or not to text Grace. She desperately wanted to see her again but also knew that every time she did, she risked her secret being discovered.

She'd also been hoping that Grace would be the one to text first, but she'd not heard a thing all day, and it was niggling at the back of her head. In the end, she put her phone away and promised herself she wouldn't text until at least the following afternoon. That sounded like a reasonable amount of time and something a normal, definitely not in love person might do. At least, she hoped so.

Chapter Twenty-five

M aybe we should discuss this over dinner?" Margot suggested. Regina's heart rate picked up in fear. They'd been working together in Margot's office most of the day, and things had been going suspiciously well. Now Regina knew why. Margot was on the charm offensive, the thing that had initially attracted Regina to her. The thing that Regina now identified as a thin veneer covering Margot's real personality.

"I don't think so," Regina said.

"A working dinner," Margot replied with a chuckle.

"I have plans."

"You have a lot of plans lately."

Regina looked straight at Margot. "Someone told me I was terribly dull."

Margot rolled her eyes. "Oh, you're not going to dredge that up, are you?"

Regina seriously considered it for a moment before discarding the idea. Margot simply wanted to have a dialogue with her that wasn't about work. And Regina was not about to give Margot anything she wanted.

"I should get back to my office. I have a few emails that I need to reply to today." Regina gathered her things and stood up.

Margot leaned back in her chair and looked up at Regina. "Amandine's Christmas party is coming up. I expect you to be there."

"I'll see." Regina wasn't about to make any promises. Spending time with Margot in a work environment was hard enough—the Christmas party would be far worse. Arjun had already mentioned the party to her, saying that not a year went by without multiple scandals taking place. He'd advised her to steer clear, and she fully intended to take his advice.

"Not a suggestion," Margot said. "Everyone is expected to make an appearance. It wouldn't look good for someone so senior and new to the firm to not show up."

Regina sighed. "Fine. I'll stay for a drink or two. When is it?"

"Two weeks away."

"Why so soon before Christmas?"

"The industry is packed with parties in December, and we have to attend as many as possible to press the flesh."

Regina wanted to gag at the tone Margot used. No doubt Margot thought it was attractive, but Regina couldn't help but see it as desperate. Suddenly, the penny dropped.

"We?"

"Yes. You're a director for Amandine. You'll be expected to attend a number of parties to network. Don't worry, I'll be by your side to show you the ropes. Arjun will receive a list in the next day or so."

Regina felt a shiver run along her spine. Spending the day with Margot was bad enough. Attending parties of an evening with her would be a nightmare. Margot had made it clear that she was waiting for Regina to rekindle their relationship, something that Margot seemed to think would simply be a matter of time.

As deluded as she was, even Margot would soon realise that time wasn't coming and would no doubt feel rejection that would soon morph into anger. And with more time together, in close quarters, that time would come sooner than Regina would have liked.

"Great," she said. "I'll look out for that schedule."

She swept out of the room before Margot could drop any further bombshells. She took the stairs to work out a little of her anger before arriving at her office.

"Welcome back," Arjun said. "I've added the next batch of

photo shoots to your calendar. I had to move a couple of other meetings—let me know if the new times don't work."

"I'll take a look, thank you."

Once she sat at her desk, she let out a long sigh. Margot was on her back, and the next series of shoots were just days away. Amandine kept giving. She reminded herself of the pay and the lack of alternatives.

She retrieved her personal phone from her bag, wondering if Grace had left a message. The screen showed her screensaver, one of the standard options that came with the phone. Disappointment flooded her at the lack of notifications. She decided to check her personal email while she had her phone to hand. Her eyebrows rose as she caught sight of something interesting. She opened the email from a recruitment consultant who she had been speaking to. She then covered her mouth to stop herself from crying out with excitement.

She had an interview. It was a senior marketing position working for an international bank. A nice, boring bank. She skimmed through the details, a smile spreading with every line she read. It sounded perfect. She quickly replied with a confirmation that she was interested and could make time whenever the hiring manager was free to see her.

The desire to jump for joy was barely contained. She did however decide to text Grace the good news.

Hi! Thought I'd let you know the good news...I have an interview!

She read the short message a couple of times and then hit the send button. She wanted to say more but decided to keep it short. Her paranoia had been working overtime for a while, and there was a part of her that worried Grace had picked up on her feelings and that was why she hadn't texted her yet. She stared at the screen for a few moments, waiting to see if the message status turned to *read*.

A minute passed and she gave up. She put her phone on her desk, face up so she'd see any replies the moment they came in. She opened a new web browser on her laptop and started to research the bank and the position.

A few minutes passed when her phone lit up with a reply from Grace. She snatched up the phone.

That's great news! You'll get it, I know you will! When is it?

Regina quickly typed back a message to say she didn't know yet and it was still being scheduled. She hesitated a second before deciding to take the plunge and ask if Grace was free that evening to meet up for a drink. The moment she sent the message, she placed the phone upside down on her desk, fearing the answer. Then she turned it the right way up because she needed to know what the answer was. Then she stood and paced behind her desk.

This was why falling in love was such a nightmare for her. Hiding her feelings was like trying to hold back a river with some tiny twigs.

The screen lit up and she grabbed her phone.

I can't, I have plans tonight. Might be able to do tomorrow or the day after, I'll look at my schedule and get back to you!

Regina slumped into her chair. The disappointment took the air from her lungs in a way she hadn't expected. It wasn't surprising to her that Grace would have plans. Regina was the sort of person who didn't have plans that evening. Grace was far too young, fashionable, and social to be at a loose end.

While Grace was all Regina could think about, it made sense that Regina was just one of many people in Grace's life, as much as that thought hurt. She fired back a quick reply to say she would be free tomorrow and that she'd wait to hear from Grace.

She dropped her phone back into her bag. Excitement about the interview evaporated as quickly as it had arrived. Of course, she was still thrilled to have the interview. Any chink of a possibility of escaping Amandine was wonderful news. But she wanted to share her joy with Grace.

"Stop this," she whispered to herself. "Focus on the interview. You can be lovestruck later."

Sitting up straight, she pulled the laptop closer and continued her research, determined to be the most prepared candidate the hiring manager would speak to.

Chapter Twenty-six

A s you'll see from my work experience, I took over that team and turned things around within six months," Regina said. "I very much enjoyed that role because of the challenges involved. I was given the tools I needed, and so it was simply down to hard work and a good strategy."

Her interviewer, Kathy, had long ago lowered her pen and was instead listening intently to Regina's words with a smile on her face. Regina had hired enough people to know that was generally a good sign. Abandoning note-taking either meant you knew the candidate was wrong or you felt you didn't need to benchmark them against other candidates since you had no question of their suitability. The smile and positive body language indicated it was the latter.

The interview had been set up for just two days after the recruitment consultant had contacted her about the position and the hiring manager's eagerness to speak with her. As it turned out, Kathy had been interviewing for the position for a while and had been struggling to fill it. The consultant indicated that Kathy was becoming frustrated with the lack of qualified candidates and wanted hiring to be over and done with as soon as possible.

It was another thing that Regina could relate to. Sometimes the right candidate came along and you snapped them up, and other times you found yourself interviewing for weeks and even months. She remembered a marketing executive role that she felt for sure was cursed after offering it to three consecutive people who all turned down the role for different reasons. She felt she was never going to escape the CV reviewing and interviewing cycle.

Kathy looked relieved in a way that told Regina she might just have the interview in the bag. Not that she would relax until she knew for sure.

"That's great," Kathy said. She glanced at the CV again. "You've told me a lot about your past experience, but we haven't spoken much about Amandine. I can see you've not been there long. Why are you looking to move to a new role now?"

"Amandine is a temporary stopgap following the collapse of Precision Marketing," Regina explained in a way she had practiced in front of a mirror just hours ago. She knew that a work history with periods of short-term employment didn't look favourable. But as long as she had a good reason for her couple of months in Amandine, then she should be able to not set off any alarm bells. "I'm enjoying my time there, but I'm looking forward to getting back into my comfort zone in the B2B world."

Regina smiled and waited. She'd answered the question, but she'd not gone into too much detail and she'd not technically lied.

"Wonderful, that's all the questions I have. Do you have any questions for me?" Kathy asked.

Regina asked the two pre-prepared questions she'd come up with. In reality, she didn't care about the answers but she knew to have a couple of questions ready to show that she had a genuine interest in the role. One was about working practices and the other about results expected from her over the next six months should she be successful. Each question was designed to show her ability to easily fit in and work towards company-specified goals.

Once Kathy had answered and Regina had confirmed she had no further questions, Kathy leaned back in her chair and nodded to herself.

"I'll be honest with you, Regina. I think you're a great fit for this role, and I'd like to offer it to you, via your recruitment consultant of course."

Regina stilled herself. She felt like jumping out of her chair with glee and relief but she needed to show professionalism for a few more minutes.

"That's wonderful to hear," she said. "I feel that this would be a great fit for me."

Kathy beamed at the confirmation. "Perfect. I do need to make you aware of our screening process. As we're a bank, there's a little more due diligence involved. We'll need to perform a criminal record check and a financial background check. Is that something you'd be comfortable with?"

"Absolutely. I had to do the same for certain clients when I worked at Precision. I completely understand."

Kathy looked relived. "Oh good. I know it can be a little bit too much of an ask for some people. We'll also need a letter of recommendation from your current line manager."

Regina's heart skipped a beat. "Not HR?"

"No. We find that some HR companies just produce letters on demand, often with no knowledge of that individual. We changed our policy last year following some previous incidents. Now we want to hear from someone who knows the individual and has worked with them personally. We find the line manager is the best reference to have."

Regina knew the colour had drained from her face by the way Kathy frowned.

"Will that be a problem?"

Regina knew she had to come clean. She wanted this job, and Kathy wanted her to have it. Margot was the only thing standing in the way, and if she was honest about the situation, then maybe there was a chance that Kathy would be willing to bend procedure for her.

"I'm afraid it will be a problem. My direct line manager is also my ex and can be rather unprofessional. She's not looking forward to my leaving Amandine, and I'm almost positive she would not give a positive reference."

"Ah. I see." Kathy nodded. "I'm sorry you're in that situation. That must be tricky?"

"Not really," Regina lied. "It's work and I rise above personal matters. But that's not quite true of her. If the role is contingent on her reference, then I think it best to tell you now that I can't guarantee what she'll say or do."

Regina was gambling that Kathy's desire to be done with interviewing and have her new hire in the bag would twist her arm to change the hiring procedure. If she had the power to do that.

"I see. I'll have to have a conversation with our HR director," Kathy said. Her expression had changed from one of delight to one of concern.

"I would be able to provide references from anyone at any of my other companies," Regina added. "And, in fact, other people at Amandine, I'm sure. It's just this one individual is tricky."

"That's good of you to offer, but I'm not sure if it will make a difference. Our screening process is very thorough, and HR has in the past not wanted to deviate from it. But I will certainly talk to them and get back to you as soon as possible." Kathy stood up and held out her hand. "It was lovely meeting you, Regina."

Regina stood and shook Kathy's hand. "Thank you, likewise."

She knew begging at this point would be the wrong thing to do. Kathy had to speak with someone else, and to do that she had to believe strongly that Regina was the right person for the role. She'd passed the interview, so now it was hers to lose. Anything else she said ran the risk of snatching the role from her. Her best form of defence was silence.

When she was on the train and heading back to Amandine after her quote-unquote *dental appointment,* she wondered if maybe she could negotiate with Margot, a thought that lasted only seconds in her head before she actually laughed out loud to herself. Margot would never do her such a favour. Her only hope now was a change in policy at the bank, something Kathy seemed uncertain could happen.

Which left Regina wondering if she would ever be able to escape Margot's clutches.

CHAPTER TWENTY-SEVEN

Regina stepped into Mister Beans and immediately noticed Grace sitting at the table they had sat at just a couple of days earlier. Grace waved excitedly.

"How did it go?"

Regina crossed the cafe and pulled out a chair.

"Good and bad," she said.

Grace gestured to the cup on the table. "I got you tea, but if you want something else I can—"

"No, no. Thank you. This is perfect." Regina shrugged out of her coat and took a sip of tea. She'd walked home in the chilly cold wind at quite a clip, and her face felt so cold it almost hurt.

"Why good and bad?" Grace asked, taking a sip from her own beverage, some fancy coffee concoction with plenty of coloured layers presented in a tall glass.

"I practically have the job, but the screening process is going to be a problem because they want a reference from Margot."

Grace sighed. "And she won't give you a reference?"

"I'm not sure what she'll do," Regina admitted. "But she's hardly known for her generous spirit. And she likes having me under her thumb, so helping me to leave Amandine wouldn't be in her best interests."

"Is there an alternative?"

"The hiring manager is going to speak to the director of HR and find out." Regina shook her head in despair. "I'm so close to being out of there but there's a chance it could all fall apart. My emotions are all over the place with this."

"I'm not surprised. I'm glad the interview part went well, though. Whatever happens, at least you know that you know how to ace an interview."

"That's true, I guess."

"When will you find out more?"

"I don't know. Soon, I hope. Although it is the weekend now, so I'll have to wait out the next couple of days."

Regina hated that the weekend was upon them. Usually she was relieved to be out of Amandine for two whole days, but now she didn't want the business world to take its well-deserved break. She wanted news and she wanted it as soon as possible. Should she be celebrating or commiserating? Would she stoop to begging Margot to help her? Would Margot flat out refuse, as she suspected would be the case? There was simply too much swimming around her head, outcomes she couldn't yet fathom swirling.

"I'm sorry. I'm afraid I'm going to be poor company tonight," Regina confessed.

"That's okay, I'm the same," Grace said.

Regina frowned at the thought that Grace was also having a bad day.

"I'm sorry to hear that, what's wrong?"

Grace fidgeted in her seat a little but remained silent for a beat. The break in eye contact gave Regina the opportunity to look at her companion a little closer. Her shoulders were slumped slightly, and her hair was down and covering her face a little.

"Oh, nothing, just a long day."

Regina didn't buy it. She was about to further question Grace when she heard a loud thumping on the window of the cafe. She turned in her seat to see a group of teenage boys outside. Two were pointing towards Grace, one was performing an obscene hand gesture, and another was banging on the glass.

Regina couldn't believe what she was seeing. She knew full well that teenage boys could often be disgraceful, especially in groups, but she'd never seen it with her own eyes. Grace was an extremely attractive woman, and the boys had clearly noticed and wanted to make some noise about it. Regina felt a wave of protectiveness come over her.

The barista, a different one from the night before, rushed to the front of the store and shouted for the boys to move on. Regina made a move to stand up, but Grace reached out for her arm.

"Don't. Please. It makes them worse."

"But—"

"Please," Grace whispered.

Regina nodded and sat back down. The barista had now opened the door and the wolf-whistling and crude comments could be heard all the clearer.

Grace kept her head ducked and ignored the comments, even though it was clear she could hear them. Regina knew there would be no chance of speaking over them or trying to pretend that nothing was happening. And so, they sat in silence and waited as the barista tried to move them along and threatened to call the police.

Eventually, after what seemed like hours but was only a couple of minutes, the boys walked on.

"I'm sorry about that," the barista said to Grace.

"No. I'm sorry," Grace replied.

"Do you ladies maybe want to sit in the booth at the back? You'll have some more privacy there."

Grace looked to Regina, her gaze hopeful.

"Sounds like a great idea, thank you," Regina said. She stood and gathered her things. The barista grabbed their drinks and walked them over to a booth at the back of the store. It was out of the way and couldn't be seen from the big glass-windowed frontage of the cafe.

They sat down, and the barista apologised once more before leaving them alone.

"Sorry about that," Grace said.

Regina shook her head. "Absolutely nothing for you to apologise for. Let's get back to where we were. You were about to tell me the real reason for you feeling down."

A hint of a smile curled at Grace's lip. "That obvious?"

"I like to think I know you," Regina admitted.

Grace pulled her drink closer and wrapped her hands around the glass mug. "I got turned down for a job today."

"I'm sorry."

"It's not the first one. In fact, it's becoming a bit of a trend."

"Why?"

Grace paused for a moment, measuring her words. "Amandine firing me didn't go unnoticed. And now some other clients are wondering what the problem was, and they are choosing not to work with me. Some have even said they heard a rumour that I've aged out."

Regina couldn't hold back her shock. "Really? That's awful."

"I didn't take the swimwear job because of a friend—I took it because I needed the work. This business is all about whether or not you're working. If you're working, then you're in demand. If you're not, then maybe there's something wrong with you, and people will choose to avoid you. Just in case."

"I'm so sorry, that sounds tough."

Grace pushed her hair behind her ear. "I knew it would come at some point. I knew I'd eventually start to receive fewer job offers, and I'd need to back out of modelling. I just didn't expect it to happen in the space of a couple of weeks. My agent says the rumours are the most damaging. People assume Amandine thought I aged out and that's why they dropped me. Margot's been approached for comment, but she won't say anything. If she at least denied that then things would get better."

"I'm willing to make a comment," Regina said. "Just tell me what you need me to say."

Grace smiled but there was still a hint of sadness in her eyes. "I appreciate that, but it has to be Margot. She's the one people want to hear from. She makes the decisions on the models. Everyone knows it."

Regina leaned back against the booth and shook her head. "Bloody Margot. She's got her claws into both of our career chances. And it's all my fault. If it was just me, then I could accept that, but the fact she's dragged you into this is so unfair."

"It's not your fault," Grace said.

"Oh, it is. It's all my fault. I wish I could do something. You know, I think it might just be easier to give her what she wants and just damn well go to dinner with her. Just to appease her, mind you. To try to convince her to do me a favour and—"

"No!" Grace reached across the table and placed her hand on Regina's forearm. "No, you can't do that."

"But I'm sure I could convince her—"

"Regina," Grace cut her off, "you can't throw yourself to the dragon for me. As sweet as that is, I don't want you to get caught up with Margot again. I couldn't stand it."

Regina grumbled for a moment but eventually nodded in agreement.

"Let's not talk about her any more," Grace suggested.

"Agreed. She doesn't deserve our thoughts."

"Definitely not yours," Grace said. "Please, promise me you won't actually consider going back to her."

"I won't, don't worry."

Grace sagged in relief. "Good. You deserve better."

Regina smiled at that. "Thank you."

"I mean it. I know I'm not your type, and I'm sorry if I've been a little too clingy. I am trying to respect your boundaries. I just wanted to say that."

Grace could have suddenly switched to another language, and Regina would have been less confused.

"Sorry…what do you mean?"

Red hit Grace's cheeks, and she shifted on the bench she sat on. "I'm just saying that I got your message and I do respect your decision."

"What message? What decision?" Regina wondered if she'd had some sort of event which had left her with no memory of what sounded like a crucially important conversation.

Grace looked at her with puzzlement. "You want to be friends," she stated, though it sounded almost questioning.

"Yes?"

"That was the decision," Grace said.

"Was it?" Regina asked, because she was quite certain that wasn't her first choice, but she was still blinded by Grace's assertion that she'd been involved in some kind of decision-making process.

"Yes," Grace insisted. "You've been pushing me away. Ignoring every advance. You...you told Margot how ridiculous it would be for us to be together."

Her voice was a whisper, but her tone had gone up a couple of octaves. She seemed as puzzled as Regina.

"Advance?" Regina knew she sounded like a fool, asking question after question in her desperate quest to keep up with what on earth was happening.

Grace's eyes widened. "Oh...wait. You...you don't. You didn't. Haven't?"

"You've been..." Regina demanded her addled brain catch up with what was happening. She held up her hand. "Wait."

Grace clamped her mouth shut. There was an edge of panic floating between them.

Regina took a few seconds to organise her thoughts and choose her words carefully.

"Grace, I'm not good at picking up on signals. If you've been... flirting with me, I've entirely missed it."

"How could you miss it?" Grace asked, a tinge of anger edging into her tone. "I shook my hair out of a bun right in front of you. I was almost naked at the time. And again, I apologise, I didn't know how serious your issue was back then. I picked hairs off your jacket which weren't there. I took every opportunity in your office to sit right next to you. Regina, I wore just a bra and a hoodie to your office and stripped off my hoodie."

Regina felt her eyes widening. She couldn't believe she'd missed the signals.

"I made you go to dinner with me," Grace continued. "You didn't ask me out, so I literally made you go have pizza with me. And you pushed me away at every step."

"I never pushed you aw—" She stopped talking when Grace stared at her with the intensity of a laser.

"You ignored my every move. You looked away. You pushed

your seat back. You didn't come out with my friends when I offered. You practically told Margot that only a lunatic would want to sleep with me."

"I never—"

"*No, of course I'm not sleeping with Grace. There's nothing between us, don't be foolish, Margot.*" Grace repeated the words Regina had long since forgotten all about. "I threw myself at you on that walk home. You just kept walking."

"I thought you were being friendly," Regina said, knowing that it sounded like the most ridiculous thing. Grace's expression stiffened into further disbelief. She held her hand up again. "Wait."

Grace again clamped her mouth shut.

Regina struggled to catch up with what she had been told. All this time, Grace had apparently been sending signals that a blind bat would have been able to see. But Regina had been completely oblivious to them. Now, Grace was convinced that Regina had been deflecting her advances. How Regina got herself into messes like this, she would never know.

"I'm clearly a very foolish woman," Regina said, "because I did not see a single advance you made. And now you've spelt them out so clearly, I see them and I'm kicking myself. I looked away from you because I find you to be unimaginably beautiful and I didn't want to be caught staring at you. I didn't come out with you and your friends because I felt I would surely be out of place. And the words I said to Margot were poorly chosen, but I meant them, as it would be lunacy for anyone to think that you would be interested in me, not the other way around." Regina thought her words would surely soothe over any hurt feelings, so she decided to try to reclaim a little high ground. "And, if we're honest, you didn't contact me after our dinner at Sergio's."

"You didn't kiss me at the end of the night!" Grace hissed. "I was waiting and waiting. Then you said *'Night* and walked away."

Regina opened her mouth and then slowly closed it again. "You—"

"Wait." It was Grace's turn to hold up her hand. "Wait, you didn't see any of my advances as advances?"

Regina shook her head.

"You weren't rejecting me?"

Regina actually laughed at the absurdity of the thought. Grace winced, and Regina realised she'd yet again put her foot in it. She scooted out of her side of the booth and sat beside Grace. She took her hand and looked into her eyes with all the sincerity she could muster.

"I laugh at that because the very idea that I would reject you is ridiculous to me. I'd never reject you, Grace. I spend all my spare time thinking of you and cursing the fact that I have no earthly chance of being with you. If I'd cottoned on to even one of your—admittedly very obvious in hindsight—hints, I would have jumped at them. If I'd have known for certain that you had been waiting for a kiss goodnight, I wouldn't have hesitated. But I'm not one for taking chances or believing in myself. I never thought someone like you would look at someone like me twice."

"You're the kindest and most sensitive person I've ever met," Grace said. "You wear your heart on your sleeve and would help anyone. You're funny and so intelligent and professional. Why someone like you would be interested in a stupid, aging model like me is beyond me. Maybe I wasn't clear. You're the first person to show no interest in me. The first person I had to pursue. I thought I was being obvious, but maybe I wasn't."

"You're not stupid and you're certainly not old," Regina rebuked softly. "I think you're absolutely perfect."

Grace closed the gap between them and with slightly trembling hands cupped Regina's face, and then, slowly so that Regina could stop her if she wanted to, Grace kissed her. Regina forgot to breathe. The woman she had been thinking about nonstop was kissing her and those lips felt as good, and tasted as good, as they looked. Instinct and need kicked in, and she kissed back, marvelling at Grace's lips against her own. Then, blissfully, Grace's tongue against her own.

She came crashing out of the bliss when she distantly heard the sound of people talking. The unexpected noise caused them to break the kiss and peer above the high-backed booth to see what was going on.

A group of young women filtered into the coffee shop, cackling and chatting in a loud manner that indicated they were almost certainly drunk.

Grace giggled. "Maybe we shouldn't be making out in Mister Beans."

Regina felt her cheeks heat. "Maybe. But I don't regret it."

"Me neither. Let's start again, okay?" Grace sat up straight and looked at Regina casually. "Hey, Regina, I've been meaning to mention that I have a huge crush on you. Maybe we could start seeing each other romantically?"

Regina couldn't help but smile. "Actually, Grace, I'm glad you mention it because I feel the same way and that sounds wonderful."

Grace cupped Regina's face and wiped away some lipstick from her lips with her thumb. "Sorry to pounce."

"Don't be. Sorry to be so dense."

"You're not dense. Your nature is the first thing that attracted me to you. You're sweet. I can't be aware of that and not realise that's a core part of who you are." Grace looked at her watch and let out a sigh. "I'm sorry, but I need to have an early night. I have a shoot tomorrow, and the car is arriving at around five in the morning."

Regina felt herself deflate. She'd been secretly hoping for a weekend with Grace now that they had finally both come clean about their feelings. It hadn't occurred to her that Grace would be working on a Saturday.

"Dinner in the evening?" Grace asked.

"You won't be too tired?" Regina asked.

"I might be tired. But if I don't get to see you again soon, I might just burst. I feel like I've been waiting forever." Grace smiled bashfully.

"Dinner tomorrow sounds perfect to me," Regina said. Suddenly her weekend wasn't looking so grim. She'd clean her apartment and have a long bath to while away the hours.

"Maybe you could walk me home now?" Grace asked. She bit her lip and looked a little shy before adding, "And this time, know that I'll be expecting a kiss goodnight outside my building."

CHAPTER TWENTY-EIGHT

Regina rarely listened to her Spotify playlist of musicals' greatest hits. It was a playlist designed for skipping around her apartment in a state of pure joy, usually while singing into a broom handle. It had been so long that she'd scrolled through quite a lot of playlists before finding the one she was looking for.

The extended version of "You Can't Stop the Beat" was pumping through the speaker of her laptop as she deep-cleaned her apartment. The task was usually something that filled her with boredom, but now she was finding it almost enjoyable for two reasons.

First, it was something to do while counting down the hours until she saw Grace for dinner that evening. Second, there was a strong probability that Grace would be spending time in Regina's apartment in the near future, and making sure it was spotless was important.

However, that didn't mean that she wasn't happy for the distraction when her phone rang. She turned the music down and answered the call from Bess.

"Afternoon," she greeted.

"Hello, poppet. I'm just calling to remind you about dinner at Leonard's tonight. I know he caught you at a bad moment and it may have slipped your mind."

Regina slapped her forehead. "I forgot."

Bess chuckled. "I thought that might be the case."

"I…I made plans," Regina said.

"Oh."

"Grace and I are having dinner," Regina explained. "A date."

Bess squealed. "A date? Oh, Regina! That's wonderful news. You found your courage then? Was it my pep talk? I'll tell Leonard you can't make it. Don't you worry about that."

Regina bit her lip. Having dinner with Grace instead of Bess and Leonard would of course be her preference, but she didn't want to offend her aunt's new man.

"I don't want to be rude," Regina said.

"Oh, he'll understand. But don't leave it too long until you bring her to see me, okay?"

Regina chuckled. "We only really started dating last night."

"You'll have to tell me all about it when you're next here." The doorbell in Bess's apartment sounded. "Oh, hold on. That will be Leonard now. Hold on a moment."

Regina waited. She could hear the muffled sound of Bess and Leonard talking, but she couldn't make out any words. A few moments later, she heard Bess pick up the phone again.

"Leonard understands, but he asked me to tell you that Grace is more than welcome to join us all for dinner as well. I told him you don't want to spend your Saturday night with us old people when you have a hot date with your new girlfriend, but he insisted I extend the invitation."

Regina laughed. "It's got nothing to do with your age, as you well know. But it would be good if we could reschedule. I am sorry for forgetting."

"Not a problem, poppet. You come and see me when you get time. No rush."

They said their goodbyes, and Regina hung up the call. She turned the music back up and continued cleaning. Just a few minutes later, the phone rang again. This time it was Grace. She turned the music off and answered the phone.

"Hello, I didn't expect to hear from you today," she said.

"I'm having a break and wanted to hear your voice," Grace replied.

Regina's heart soared at the confirmation that Grace's feelings hadn't changed. Paranoia often lurked around the corner when it came to matters of the heart, but particularly now in the case of Grace. Regina had somehow managed to get everything she ever wanted, and she wasn't yet completely reassured that it wasn't going to vanish as quickly as it had arrived.

"How is your day going?" Regina asked, not trusting herself to start a conversation on how much she'd missed Grace that morning. The desire to be close to Grace had been overwhelming. Knowing that they felt the same way but had to wait to be together was maddening. Even if it was a few short hours.

"It's good. We may be done a little early if things carry on the way they are."

Regina beamed. "Well, if you have some free time, I can definitely rearrange my schedule."

"I hoped you might say that," Grace confessed. "What have you been up to?"

"Housework," Regina said. "And my aunt called. I'd forgotten that I'd been invited to Leonard's for some apparently award-winning chicken pie."

Grace chuckled. "Sounds delicious. When's that?"

"It was supposed to be tonight, but we're going to rearrange."

"You can't do that. If Leonard booked you in first—"

"Leonard will be absolutely fine to rearrange," Regina reassured. She wasn't about to let her Saturday night date with Grace slip through her fingers. "He extended the invitation to you, too. But he's also more than happy to rearrange."

"We should go," Grace said.

Regina hesitated. "Sorry?"

"We should go. He's important to her. She's important to you. Besides, I know I'll need to be approved by Bess at some point anyway—we might as well do it sooner rather than later."

"Bess will love you," Regina said.

"Well, we'll find that out tonight when we have some award-winning chicken pie."

Regina pinched the bridge of her nose. All thoughts of a romantic dinner for two flew out of her head.

"I want to meet her," Grace added. "She's the most important person in your life, and I hope to be an important person in your life, too. I know we're at the early stage of our relationship, but I'm serious about us, Regina."

Her mouth felt suddenly dry. Grace's words hit her hard. Confirmation that she wasn't the only one who had fallen head over heels was wonderful and overwhelming all at once.

"Have I said too much?" Grace asked, her voice no more than a nervous whisper.

"Not at all," Regina said quickly in a reassuring tone. "You don't have to meet Bess tonight if it's too much, but if you're certain, then I can call her back. She is important to me, you're absolutely right. But I know that she will find you as amazing as I do. There's nothing to worry about there."

"Okay," Grace said, her voice still soft. "I do also really like chicken pie."

Regina laughed. "Then I'll let them know to expect us."

Nerves vibrated from Grace in a way Regina had never seen before. Usually confident and poised, Grace was trying to keep up appearances, but her nervous laugh, lack of conversation, and overall demeanour gave her away. Regina didn't know if it was because it was their first official date or because they were meeting up with Bess. Either way, Regina hoped that meeting Bess would soon put Grace's mind at ease and show her that there was nothing to worry about after all.

They entered the reception of Calm Acres and Grace looked around with interest.

"This place is lovely. Sign me up."

"I know," Regina agreed. "It took a few attempts to find a good fit, but Bess is very happy here, and I know the staff really care for her."

Regina nodded to the receptionist and gestured for Grace to follow her down the corridor towards Bess's apartment.

"We should have brought something," Grace said. She'd previously worried aloud about her outfit, whether or not Leonard had seriously meant to invite her or if he was just being kind, and if Bess would write her off for being a young airhead.

"I asked several times, and they said not to bring anything."

"We still should have brought something." Grace paused. "I could run out and get something. A bottle of wine?"

Regina bit her lip to stop from smiling.

"What?" Grace asked.

"Nothing. I'm just surprised how nervous you are." Regina grinned. "It's adorable."

Grace playfully smacked her upper arm. "It's not."

"It is." Regina took Grace's arm and looped it through hers. "We're going to be fine. Don't worry."

They turned into the corridor where Bess's apartment was located, and Regina smiled to herself at Bess standing in the hallway waiting for them. The moment she spotted them, she walked forward with arms outstretched, walking cane suddenly forgotten.

"You must be Grace, welcome!"

Grace let go of Regina's arm and walked into the hug Bess offered. "Thank you, it's so nice to meet you."

"Come in, come in." Bess took Grace's arm and looped it around hers and led her into the apartment.

Regina stood in the empty corridor. "Hello Regina, nice to see you. Do come in. Why, thank you, I will," she muttered to herself.

"Don't stand out there being sarcastic," Bess called out. "You know the way in."

Any worries Regina had about giving up her evening to spend it with Leonard and Bess floated away. The couple fell over themselves to make Grace feel at home. Regina was almost ignored in the flurry of questions and conversation that surrounded Grace, but at no time were the questions personal or probing. A genuine smile had soon reappeared on Grace's face and told Regina that any concerns had been smoothed away.

At the dinner table, Regina sat next to Grace with Bess opposite her and Leonard opposite Grace. Grace had briefly placed her hand on Regina's thigh and squeezed it in a private message that said she was doing fine.

"How's the shrew?" Bess asked as they started eating.

Regina made a face. "Must we call her that?"

"Who?" Grace asked, intrigued.

"Margot," Bess said. "The shrew."

Grace giggled. Leonard wisely kept quiet.

"She's herself," Regina answered.

Bess nodded. "I wish I could see her again. I'd give her a good talking to."

"Well, thankfully for all involved, those days are over," Regina said. "Can we change the topic, please?"

"I have a question," Leonard said, stepping in. He looked at Grace. "Have you ever been asked to model something that's just plain ugly? Do you ever look down at yourself and think *I'd never wear this!*"

Grace smiled. "Sometimes, yes."

Leonard shook his head. "Oh, well, that's it then. I don't want to be a model. You can cancel the gig, Bess."

Bess tried to smother her smile. Grace on the other hand couldn't have smiled wider.

"Ignore his silliness," Bess said.

"I like silliness," Grace said. "You remind me of my granddad."

Leonard beamed. "Handsome fellow, right? Sharp as a tack, I'm sure."

"Absolutely," Grace said.

"Silly bugger," Bess said. "Tell me, Grace, do you like *Frost*?"

Grace frowned.

"She means the TV show *A Touch of Frost*," Regina explained. She looked at Bess. "I suspect she might be a bit young to remember that."

"Oh, that sounds a little familiar," Grace said. "But I don't think I've seen it."

Bess's eyes lit up. "Do you like detective series?"

"Yes, I used to watch *Line of Duty* with my mum all the time."

Bess practically vibrated with excitement.

Regina pointed her fork at Bess. "No. She doesn't want to binge *Frost* with you."

Bess shook her head. "You don't know that." She turned to Grace. "It is one of the greatest TV dramas of all time. *Radio Times* called it essential viewing."

"In 1995," Regina added under her breath.

"She doesn't want to watch *Frost* with you, Bess," Leonard said. "She's coming to the cinema with me. I can get us into the senior showings of all the best films. Five pounds and you get a cup of hot chocolate thrown in. It's a great deal."

"Are you both trying to poach my date?" Regina asked.

Grace laughed. "Five pounds is a pretty sweet cinema deal."

"The hot chocolate is very good," Leonard added.

"As is this chicken pie," Grace said.

Leonard couldn't have looked happier if he tried.

"It is," Regina agreed. "Thank you again for inviting us."

"Not at all. Thank you for taking the time. I know weekends are precious things when you're young," he replied.

Regina nearly laughed. She didn't feel young in the slightest. She supposed in comparison to Leonard and Bess, she was. But that didn't change the fact that she'd never really felt young. She'd often been told that she had a wise head on young shoulders. It was years later when a therapist told her that was likely a response to the trauma of losing her parents.

Old, cautious, and dull was how she saw herself. And indeed how she knew some others saw her. But for some reason, Grace didn't see her that way at all. Grace had expressed that she considered Regina settled, calm, and mature. She'd also expressed that those were qualities she found incredibly attractive in a woman.

Regina's mind drifted back to the kiss the night before. Seconds after they'd arrived at Grace's apartment, Regina had cupped her face and planted what she hoped was an unforgettable kiss on Grace's lips. Grace had melted against her in a way that Regina had previously thought impossible.

When they parted, Grace had indicated that if she wasn't due to work the next day she would have invited Regina up to her apartment.

It was done casually and with a questioning glint in Grace's eye. She wanted to gauge Regina's reaction and see if she'd gone too far too soon. Regina had been very clear in her response. If she was invited up, then she'd be the luckiest woman in the world, and if and when that moment came, she'd happily oblige.

How she could have missed so many obvious signals was beyond her. She'd been lucky to have been given another chance by fate, and she fully intended to hold on to it.

"Isn't that right, Regina?" Bess asked, in a tone that suggested she was asking for the second time.

"Sorry, my mind wandered," she confessed.

"Your father named you Regina because he wanted you to feel like a queen."

Regina smiled. "Yes. That's right."

She wasn't certain if the tactic had worked. But knowing that there was a reason behind her name beyond someone thinking it sounded nice had always given her some comfort.

Grace took hold of her arm and cuddled up against her. "I love it."

"You know, I do have a photo of her dressed up as Queen Victoria for a school play," Bess added.

Regina glared at her. "I think you must be thinking of someone else."

Bess chuckled. "Maybe. We'll have to see."

"I'd love to see any photos you have," Grace said.

Regina rolled her eyes. She knew there was no chance of escaping now—the photo albums were about to be given their annual airing.

Later, when they were gathered on the sofa and going through the photo albums, she realised how nice it was to share her past with Grace and Leonard. Both she and Bess had managed to find people who were perfect matches. She hadn't realised how lonely they must have both been until she experienced the warmth of family again.

❖

Regina and Grace walked hand in hand back from the train station. Grace revelled in the closeness. Her relationship with Regina had very nearly never happened because of miscommunication, and now she was sure to show her feelings at every available opportunity.

"That was pretty good chicken pie," Grace said.

"Very good," Regina agreed.

"He's so sweet, too," Grace added.

"He is. Except that bit where he was trying to pick you up right in front of me," Regina joked.

Grace laughed. "Five pounds for a cinema ticket, I might take him up on that."

"Don't forget the hot chocolate."

"Who could say no to an offer like that?" Grace chuckled. "Honestly, though, he is so nice and sweet. He really adores Bess."

"Yes, he does. She adores him, too. It's nice to see her in love again."

"Has she been single for long?"

"Years. Her husband died when I was very little. I don't remember him at all. Since then she's dated but never found anyone she really liked. And the only one she stayed with for any length of time ended up cheating on her."

Grace growled at the thought. "People can be so cruel."

"They can."

They approached Grace's building and stopped outside.

"So, you think she liked me?" Grace asked, a little shyly. She knew how important Bess's opinion was to Regina. The thought that Bess might object to their relationship had sat at the back of her mind like an evil seed trying to take root.

"Liked you? I think she adored you. I was barely spoken to."

Relief at the confirmation quickly gave way to the next pressing concern on Grace's mind.

"And do you like me?" Grace asked, her voice dropping suggestively.

Regina swallowed. "Yes, very much."

"Would it be wrong to ask you to come upstairs tonight?"

Regina looked at her with a smile. "Not wrong at all."

"Good, I don't want to scare you off by being direct. But it was pretty hard to not touch you for the last few hours, and I'm desperate for you."

Grace didn't care how eager she sounded. The feeling had been growing for a while. She needed Regina, and needed Regina to be absolutely clear how she felt and what she wanted. No more miscommunication, no more distance between them.

Regina quickly nodded, an underlying urgency clear in her gaze. "I feel the same way."

Grace took her hand and led her up the short flight of stairs and towards the entrance.

CHAPTER TWENTY-NINE

Regina woke up in unfamiliar surroundings, a scenario which had never happened to her before. She didn't feel afraid or unsettled—instead, an overwhelming sense of calm happiness had washed over her. It took her a few moments to piece together the events of the previous night, coming up to Grace's apartment and soon tumbling into bed.

She turned over and saw Grace sitting up in bed, scrolling on her phone.

"Morning," Regina said.

Grace's face lit up, and she dropped the phone to the bed before diving down to capture a kiss.

"Hi."

Regina imagined that her own expression mirrored Grace's— deliriously happy.

"Sorry I didn't wake you," Grace continued. She'd snuggled down into the bedding now and they lay face to face. "I thought I'd let you sleep a little longer. It is Sunday after all."

"Is it?" Regina asked, completely unaware of boring concepts such as time.

Grace giggled. "Do you have plans for today?"

"Nothing comes to mind. You?"

"Well…" Grace shuffled a little closer. "This seems nice."

Regina grinned. "It does, doesn't it."

"Stay?" Grace asked. "Unless you don't want to, of course. I know I must seem terribly clingy."

Regina silenced her with a kiss. "Not clingy at all. I'd love to stay."

Grace looked utterly relieved. "I've been looking for this for ages," she confessed.

"Looking for what?" Regina asked.

"Someone who fitted. Someone I could settle down with. I knew the moment I saw you that you were who I'd been looking for. You're calming. All the people around me are young and energetic and I can't keep up. I just want to lounge around on a Sunday and talk, read, and relax with the person I…love." Grace's expression changed when she realised she'd said the word *love*. "Too soon?"

Regina shook her head. "Not too soon. I've loved you for a while. And I don't think of love as something you switch on and off. I think it's something that grows deeper and stronger. And I'd love to spend Sunday with you, the person I've fallen in love with."

Relief flooded Grace and she threw herself closer to Regina, her ear against her chest.

"I've never been happier," Grace whispered.

Regina realised the same was true of her.

When Regina woke on Monday morning, she felt a sense of dread. Not because of any unfamiliar settings but because she knew she now had to leave the perfect bubble she and Grace had created for themselves and go out into the real world.

She picked up her phone from the bedside table and checked her email. It was a bad habit she had picked up over the years. When barely awake, the first thing she would do was scroll through first her personal and then her work emails. It was hardly the best way to start the day, and today would be no exception.

"Damn," she mumbled.

"Hmm?" Grace queried, half asleep beside her.

"Sorry, nothing," Regina whispered.

Grace wrapped her arm around Regina's middle. "Don't fib. What's wrong?"

"The hiring manager has emailed," Regina explained. "The HR Director won't authorise a change of policy. They want a reference letter from Margot."

"Maybe she'll do it," Grace said. "She must know it's not tenable to keep you at Amandine forever."

"I'm not so certain." She lay on her back, and Grace positioned herself to rest her head on her chest. "I think she wants to ruin me."

"She can't," Grace said softly. "I won't allow it."

Regina smiled. "I'm sorry but I don't think you get much say in it."

"We can manage whatever Margot wants to throw at us."

Regina hesitated. She didn't want to ruin a beautiful morning, wrapped up with the woman she loved, with the cold harsh realities of the world. But she also couldn't remain silent and pretend that everything would be okay.

"If I lose this job, Bess will be homeless. And, I suppose, I'll be as well—but more pressingly, Bess."

"If you lose the Amandine job, I'll pay for Bess's care. And you can move in here," Grace said sleepily. "We can manage."

Regina glanced down at Grace in surprise. "I can't ask you to do that."

"You've not asked me. I've offered."

"It's a not a small amount of money."

"I've been saving for retirement since I was twenty-one," Grace said. "You never know when modelling gigs will vanish. I can afford it."

Regina remained silent for a moment as she allowed that to sink in.

"It's not an offer that I'll retract if we...don't...I mean, if anything changes," Grace added, her voice suddenly very soft. "If you change your mind."

Regina placed a finger under Grace's chin and encouraged her to look up. "I'm not changing my mind. You'll have to get rid of me with a crowbar."

Grace beamed and stretched up to kiss her.

"But I can't accept your offer," Regina added.

"Why not?"

"Because…" Regina failed to come up with a reason she could verbalise. "Because, I can't."

"That's not a reason."

"I know."

"Because I don't want to change things between us," Regina said, feeling that the words weren't sufficient but explained some of what she was thinking.

"Well, I don't want Bess or you to be homeless. Besides, we're talking about a maybe scenario. We don't need to decide anything now. Just know that you have a safety net. If you want one."

Regina opened her mouth to reply, to decline Grace's offer for a second time. But instead she closed her mouth again and slowly nodded. Being in a relationship like this felt new and different. Even before her disastrous relationship with Margot, Regina had never been with someone who made her feel the way Grace did. There was no scheming, no upper hand to be won, no insecurities.

She felt in love and loved, completely. Even in such a short period of time, they'd both dropped any pretence and fallen into a partnership where they could rely on the other to catch them if necessary. It would take some time to get used to, but she looked forward to the journey. She kissed the top of Grace's head and mulled over her options.

❖

The walk to the office gave Regina time to consider her options. She wanted the job at the bank, not just because it was an alternative to Amandine but because she felt it was something she would be good at. It would also be a relief to go to work and not be frightened of being placed in a situation that would trigger her anxiety, there being very few half-naked models working for banks.

The only way to seal the deal would be to ask Margot for a favour, one that Margot was unlikely to give, and one that would show Regina's hand that she'd been searching for other jobs. Margot's strange and unpredictable behaviour made it impossible to predict what she might do. Would she concede defeat, ruin Regina's chances, or throw her into yet another impossible situation designed by revenge and anger?

Her thoughts were interrupted by an incoming call from Bess. "Hello?"

"Hello, poppet."

"Everything okay?" Regina asked.

"Yes. I'm calling, as per your instructions, to request permission before I go ahead and give someone your phone number."

Regina breathed a sigh of relief, partly for the call being innocuous in nature and partly for Bess finally getting the message that randomly handing out people's phone numbers simply wasn't the done thing any more.

"To who?" Regina asked.

"Nick."

"Who?"

"Leonard's grandson."

Prompted, Regina remembered the hoodie-wearing young man but couldn't fathom why he might want to get in touch.

"Do you know why he wants my number?"

"No."

Regina rolled her eyes. "Well, okay, I guess."

She hoped it wasn't some request for a double dating situation, or a chance for Nick to warn Regina about some terrible secret of Leonard's. She had enough going on without adding that to her concerns.

"Okay, poppet, thank you." Bess hung up the call before Regina had a chance to say anything else.

Regina looked at the phone in surprise for a moment before shaking her head.

Regina pocketed her phone and let out a sigh. It had to be about Leonard. She dreaded some awful piece of news coming her way, something she had to pass along to Bess. Maybe Leonard was married. Or ill. She shook her head to remove the negative thoughts. Maybe Nick simply wanted to organise a secret birthday party or some kind of family dinner. It didn't have to be a bad thing, she reminded herself. Even if that was often where her thoughts led her straight out of the gate.

She looked up at the office building in front of her. Amandine HQ towered over her, and she felt a shiver run up her spine that was nothing to do with the winter weather.

❖

Margot laughed. At first it was a soft laugh of disbelief. Then it built into something that neared a manic episode. Regina bit the inside of her cheek and looked away. So much for appealing to Margot's kind nature. If it had ever existed it was now buried so deeply within her that it was unlikely to ever be found again.

"You expect me to write you…what? A glowing reference? Come now, Regina. Did you honestly think there was the remotest chance that I would do that? For you?"

"Not particularly," Regina confessed. "But I had to ask. I think if you really consider this, you'll see that it's the best solution for all of us."

"I don't think it's a very good solution at all," Margot said. "No, I rather enjoy having you here. I don't see any reason why I should help you to leave. If you're to leave this place, Regina, it's because you quit—which we both know you won't do because of that old aunt of yours—or because I sack you. Which, at the moment, it wouldn't please me to do."

"This power crazed attitude has to stop, Margot."

"I'm not power crazed. I simply know better than you." Margot picked up a magazine from her desk. "Besides, if they won't hire you without a pinkie promise from your manager that you're good at your job, then do they even want you?"

Regina bit her tongue. It was a ridiculous policy—that couldn't be denied. But Kathy had indicated they'd had a problem in the past which had instigated the need.

"And it wouldn't look good on me if you left now. I did personally vouch for you, remember?"

"To torment me," Regina reminded her. "Wouldn't you be

happier to let me go and forget about me? You could move on with your life."

Margot silently opened the magazine and started leafing through the pages.

"You're going to ignore me?" Regina asked after a few moments of silence.

"I'm giving you an opportunity to go and pretend this never happened," Margot said. "Leave now and I'll forget that you've been hunting for jobs under my nose."

"You can't honestly be surprised that I didn't want to remain under your control like this. Margot, come on. You've trapped me here, indicated that you think I'll somehow change my mind and we'll reunite—which I again emphasise will not happen—and have seemingly enjoyed making my life miserable by having me attend photo shoots you know I'll find uncomfortable. Let's end this all now."

"No!" Margot looked up at her with eyes blazing. "No. Now get out."

Regina looked over the woman before her. Reasoning with her was clearly never going to work. Any common sense that Margot had once possessed seemed to have been swallowed up. Regina didn't want to waste time analysing what trauma her captor was going through. All she knew was that she was trapped by a madwoman. She stood up and left the office.

At first, she had intended to go to her own office. But once she was in the stairwell, she continued walking to the ground floor, through reception, and out into the London streets. She'd left her bag and coat in her office, which was probably a good thing or else she doubted she'd ever return and then where would she be? The cold wind whipped around her, but she didn't care as she walked on autopilot towards St. James's Park. It was all she could think to do. The comforting surroundings of the place she had always gone to whenever she needed space called to her.

Chapter Thirty

Regina paced around the park, trying to keep warm. She couldn't stay under Margot's thumb anymore. It was untenable. The woman was deranged. But then she acted like that because she knew she held all the cards. The circular argument had been going round and round her head for the last hour as she'd circled the park in the hope that she'd be able to find a resolution.

"Hi."

Regina stopped and turned to see Grace smiling at her. Regina blinked in surprise. She'd not told Grace or indeed anyone where she was.

"Arjun called me," Grace said. "He said you went to see Margot and never came back. Margot's PA said you left the office like you were going to commit a murder." She held out Regina's coat. "He also said that you didn't have a coat with you. So I stopped by Amandine and picked it up."

Regina gratefully put the coat on. She'd been shivering for a while, and it was only her stubborn nature that had kept her out in the cold.

"How did you know where to find me?"

"You told me you come here when work gets hectic. I thought it might be hectic today," Grace said. She took hold of Regina's arm and tugged. "Come on, let's walk and try to warm up."

"How did Arjun know to call you?" Regina asked.

"You're full of questions." Grace chuckled. "He assumed we

were a couple ages ago, even though I told him we weren't. When you left the office and didn't answer his calls, he got worried, so he called me. Do you want to tell me what happened?"

Regina shook her head. "There's not a lot to say. I tried to reason with Margot but she can't be reasoned with. I'm not going to escape her any time soon. In fact, now that I've tipped her off that I'm actively looking for work, I wouldn't be surprised if she did something else."

"Like what?"

"I don't know. I honestly can't predict what she'll do next. She's always been domineering, selfish, and ruthless. But this is beyond anything I thought she was capable of."

Grace remained silent. She held on to Regina's arm as they slowly walked through the park. Regina felt strengthened by her presence. Having Grace come and find her in her moment of need filled her with joy, which smashed up against the residual anger from her altercation with Margot.

Her phone rang, and thinking it was a worried Arjun, she pulled it out of trouser pocket. A number she didn't recognise appeared on the screen. She watched it ring.

"What are you waiting for?" Grace asked.

"I don't know who it is." Regina saved every number she received or dialled. It meant her contact list was enormous, but it also meant she was never caught on calls with salespeople or scammers.

"Well, you'll never know who it is if you don't answer it," Grace said. She reached up and swiped to answer the call.

Regina hurriedly put the phone to her ear.

"Hello?"

"Hey, is that Regina?" a male voice asked.

"It is."

"Hey, it's Nick. Leonard's grandson. How are you doing?"

Regina barely resisted the urge to sigh. The last thing she needed was whatever situation Nick was about to throw at her.

"Hello, Nick. I'm well, thank you. You?" She kept her tone as disinterested as she felt. Whatever Nick needed, he couldn't have picked a worse time.

"I'm great. Look, I'll cut to the chase. My granddad said you were looking for a new job, and it just so happens I need a marketing director. We've been on the lookout for a few months, but no one has really fit the bill or wanted to take the risk. We're a start-up in AI, and we're in competition against some big names. But we have some incredible data scientists and programmers, we just don't have the marketing brain in-house yet. We need to package and sell the product. Literally starting from scratch. I looked at your LinkedIn profile, and you have tons of great experience. And you worked with Terry Bradley, who I know really well, and he said you're a genius. I was wondering if you'd be interested in this sort of thing? We can have a chat."

Regina opened and closed her mouth a couple of times. Whatever she'd been expecting from Nick, it certainly hadn't been that. But before she got too excited, she knew she needed to get some more information.

"That does sound very interesting. And AI is a tremendously fast-paced industry, so I can understand the need for a strong marketing director. So that I don't waste any of your valuable time, what salary range are you thinking for the right candidate?"

Nick reeled off the financials, talking about the funding his company had gotten from various seed investors. He spoke about the salary, benefits package, and share equity, all of which exceeded Regina's expectations and would put her in a very comfortable position.

"But it's risky," Nick added. "I want to be upfront. We're working hard to make it work, but we don't have the backing some of these firms do. We can't pour twenty million a month into advertising. We need to be creative. We have a budget. I think it's a good budget. But there's still that risk."

Risk. The word shook Regina. She didn't know if she could take a risk. She'd avoided them her entire life, and hearing someone specifically say that the situation was risky had activated a fear reaction within her.

"Nick, can I call you back? This sounds fascinating, but I have another call coming in which I have to take," she lied.

"No problem. Give me a call if this sounds like something you're interested in, and we can meet."

Regina said she'd consider it and then said goodbye and hung up the call.

She stood still and worried her lip. Grace looked at her with concern.

"What is it?"

"That was Nick, Leonard's grandson. He's offering me a job. Well, I think it's an interview for a job."

A smile spread across Grace's face like lightning before quickly turning into a frown.

"Why are you not celebrating this?"

"It's a start-up. A risky one." Regina looked around and spotted a park bench. She walked them over to it and took a seat. Her heart was racing, and she couldn't feel any residual traces of cold. No, now she was burning up. The idea of jumping from Amandine to a bank was one thing. But jumping to a risky start-up was something entirely different.

She'd worked for agencies who partnered with start-ups. They were scrappy, chasing their own tail, and prone to failure. Many, many failed. It wasn't what she wanted. She wanted security and safety.

"What did he say?" Grace asked.

Regina relayed the conversation. Grace listened intently and thought for a few moments before saying, "Well, I don't know much about business. But I know that working with Nick would be better than working with Margot. Isn't it just as risky to be working at Amandine? You're at the mercy of Margot's moods. At least at the start-up you're at the mercy of investors, money, and sales figures. And you're working with a team of people who want to succeed. Not battling day after day with one person."

"Margot may talk the talk, but she doesn't have that much power," Regina explained. "She can't make a decision to sack me without speaking with other people and going through a complicated process. Yes, I'll battle her every day, but there's more job security at Amandine."

Regina worried her lip and shook her head as she thought through the situation.

Grace waited patiently. She took hold of Regina's hand, and Regina felt a wave of comfort flowing through the connection.

"He said it was risky," Regina said.

"Yes?" Grace prompted.

"I'm…well, I'm frightened," she confessed. "I've not been able to face risks ever since my parents died in an accident. It cemented this fear in me that terrible things can happen when you take a risk. I know that sounds ridiculous, but they died in a ski lift accident. My mother had always been interested in skiing, but they'd never gone. They were both middle-aged when they decided to take a risk and go. My father actually joked about coming back with broken bones. I didn't realise then that there was even a possibility they might never come back at all."

Grace threw her arms around Regina and held her close.

"And now I have this fear of taking chances. I'm always worried about what might go wrong."

"You took a chance on us," Grace whispered.

"And it terrified me."

"But you did it."

Regina considered that for a moment. She had taken a risk, and it had worked out. In fact, so far, it had been the best decision of her life. Walking the quiet path might have been safe, but it hadn't led to much joy or excitement in her life. The first time she really took a risk was in telling Grace how she felt, and now she was the luckiest woman alive.

"At least find out more," Grace said. "Maybe he's overselling the riskiness?"

"Maybe," Regina mused.

"Whatever happens, I'll be here to catch you," Grace said. She kissed Regina's hair and leaned back so she could make eye contact. "Even if it's just emotionally. I'm here for you."

Regina wiped a stray tear from her face and tried to force a smile. "Thank you."

She took a deep breath and thought for a few moments before

nodding. "You're right. I should call him back and get some more information. I can't make a decision without all the information."

"Cool. Meet with him today," Grace pressed.

"I have to get back to the office," Regina said. The idea filled her with dread.

"No, you're out sick for the rest of the day," Grace said with a grin. "I told Arjun."

Regina laughed. "And what made you think I'd want to take the day off?"

"I thought you might want to. And if you didn't, you could always go in anyway. Miraculous recovery or something."

Regina kissed Grace on the cheek. "Thank you."

She called Nick back and asked if he had any availability that day. He said he'd clear his diary and could meet her whenever, which Regina took to be a sign of desperation, equally good news and bad. She arranged a time and a location for later that afternoon.

Off the call, she said to Grace, "Right, I need to research everything there is to know about AI in three hours."

Grace's eyebrows shot up. "Is that even possible?"

"Who knows? Let's find a cafe."

Chapter Thirty-one

Regina woke up with a start. Grace quickly sat up and placed a comforting hand on her naked back.

"Are you okay?"

She took a few moments to control her breathing. "Yes, just a nightmare."

Grace shuffled forward so they could see one another. Regina leaned against Grace, thankful for the comfort she could draw. It had been a long time since she'd had someone to turn to when the nightmares came.

"Want to talk about it?" Grace asked.

The nightmare had tossed and turned its way through her psyche, taking inspiration from the ups and downs of the previous day. From arguing with Margot, to telling Kathy that she wouldn't be able to provide a reference and would need to withdraw her application, to chatting casually with Nick over hot drinks in a trendy cafe, it had been a day that she needed to process.

Unfortunately, that processing had come in the form of nightmares. Being stuck with Margot breathing down her neck to suddenly working with Nick and being happy only to find out the money had run out. The life decision was in front of her, and even her nightmares didn't know what she'd do.

Nick had been very upfront about the risks. Maybe a little too upfront. Part of her salary would be tied up in stock options, options that would never materialise if the company folded before a certain date. The office was cramped, and he couldn't promise her a permanent desk or even access to a meeting room. The product was finished and ready for launch but that was all that could be said. She'd have to start from scratch. Branding, pricing, strategy, and tracking. Nothing was in place. They didn't even have a website. And she'd not have any help. She'd be alone and against the clock.

On the flipside, she'd be paid well as long as the company was afloat. She'd manage her own time and work with no one looking over her shoulder.

"I still don't know what to do," Regina said.

They'd spent the evening together, Regina running over the same pros and cons of both jobs over and over again and Grace patiently listening to her. It kept coming back to the same thing. It made sense for Regina to work with Nick, but it also scared her more than she could say.

Grace smothered a yawn. "Can I ask a question?"

"Of course."

"Is knowing you'll be miserable at Amandine worth *possibly* being miserable elsewhere?"

Regina thought for a while. It was a fair enough question. She knew what Amandine would bring. The other option was a gamble. The business would either fly or fail. But the fear was overwhelming her.

"Could this be a case where the fear of something going wrong might be worse than it actually going wrong?" Grace added. "Might you not be a little in shock after losing your job at Precision and being put in this situation to begin with?"

That was it, she realised. She was in shock. She was still processing what had happened before and living in a state of fear. She'd never had time to stop and think about what had happened with Precision and process the loss of her old life. It had been snatched away in a moment, and she'd been living in fear ever since. It lurked at the back of her brain, telling her that she might lose everything again at any minute and to stick to the safest possible path. Even when that wasn't the logical thing to do.

"You're right," she whispered. "This job, no matter how risky, isn't as risky as staying at Amandine. I need to tell Nick I'll take the job."

Grace squeezed Regina tightly. "Good. I really think that's the right decision. I hate the idea of you being around Margot for a moment longer than you have to."

"I'll tell her I'm leaving," Regina said.

"Of course."

"In person," Regina clarified.

Grace leaned back and frowned. "Is that a good idea?"

"It's the right thing to do," Regina said. "Once I've spoken to Nick and ironed out the details, I'll go and see Margot and tell her that we need to cut ties for good."

Grace looked down at the bedsheets and nodded, a tiny pout on her face. "You're right. It's the right thing to do." She looked up. "I love that about you."

Regina pulled Grace into a hug. "Thank you for listening to me while I worked through all of this. I'm sorry I've handled this so badly."

"You haven't. You're just working through some things." Grace kissed her cheek. "You'll learn one day that taking the plunge can lead to really good things."

Regina nodded. "Like you." She turned and looked at the alarm clock on the bedside table. "Oh dear, it's too late to go back to sleep and too early to get up. Whatever shall we do?"

Grace didn't need much convincing and clamped her lips to Regina's and pushed her down into the soft, warm sheets.

❖

"Feeling better?" Margot asked when Regina walked into her office a few hours later. "I heard you were unwell yesterday after our meeting."

The smirk on Margot's face indicated that she didn't much care for Regina's well-being. In fact, it looked distinctly as if she found the whole thing amusing.

Regina closed the door behind her. She stood in front of Margot's desk and prepared herself to deliver her news. Acknowledging that her fear was real and valid, while also being suffocating and making her almost unable to balance her options, was freeing.

She no longer cared what Margot did. She was leaving Amandine, and if the start-up brought failure, then that would be a bridge she would cross when it came. A weight had been lifted, and she could see a future away from this possessive woman. And that future was bright.

"I'm leaving," Regina said.

Margot laughed. "You're not."

"I am. As soon as I've spoken to you, I'll be handing in my pass and my laptop, and I'll be leaving immediately."

Margot narrowed her eyes and gave Regina a glare she knew well. But beneath it was the tiniest flicker of hesitation.

"You want to throw away your career?"

"No. I'm finally in a situation where I can put some much-needed distance between us. Margot, what you're doing, what you've done, it isn't right. You must know that."

Margot jumped to her feet. "All I've done is give you a job. Picked you up from the gutter and given you a chance!"

"You brought me here knowing that this job would be hard for me, to make me struggle with something you always saw as my odd weakness. You put me in a position where I had to report to you. You've suggested that we might one day get back together, which is sheer madness—"

"I never—"

"You did! Enough with the rewriting history, Margot."

Margot snorted a laugh. "You're delusional."

"No. I'm not. And you trying to convince me otherwise is not going to change the fact that you've been using your power over people and acting wholly inappropriately. Probably because you're worried about getting older and how you look."

"Don't say another word," Margot ground out.

"You've had work done." Regina gestured to her face. "And I think you're not happy with it. I think you're surrounded by people who think that fashion and looks come first. You're in an industry that can swallow people up if they have even the slightest hesitation about their looks. I think—"

"Stop!" Margot smashed her hand down on the desk.

"I fully intend to stop. I'm going to stop working here. Stop walking on eggshells around you. Stop allowing you to control me. Stop allowing you to put me in compromising situations for your own amusement." Regina stood a little taller. "And stop you from interfering with my relationship with Grace."

Margot's face froze.

"You see, I wasn't in a relationship with her at first. When I told you there was nothing between us, that was the truth. But we're together now."

Regina couldn't help but enjoy the look of horror on Margot's face. In fact, considering the hell Margot had put her through, she thought it only fair that she really rub salt in the wound.

"Actually, I'm happy. Really, genuinely happy, for the first time in a long time." Regina smiled. "I should thank you, I suppose. Without your little scheme, I would never have met Grace. She's the best thing that ever happened to me."

"Get out," Margot whispered.

"With absolute pleasure." Regina turned on her heel and walked out of Margot's office for the last time.

She'd come to speak to Margot face to face in the hope that she could defuse the animosity that was lodged between them. But instead she'd managed to get the verbal upper hand, something she didn't regret. Margot was a bitter and twisted individual, and while Regina might have wanted the best for everyone, there was a little part of her that was happy to see Margot suffer for her actions.

She walked to the other end of the office to speak with Sheila, the head of design, and someone Regina only knew in passing.

She knocked on the open door, "Hi, do you have a minute?"

Sheila was a larger-than-life woman who always seemed to have a huge smile on her face. Everyone had a nice thing to say about her, and Regina had often wished she reported into Sheila rather than Margot.

"Sure, come in," Sheila said. "How can I help?"

"I'm just saying goodbye," Regina said. "I'm off to another role."

Surprised, Sheila blinked a few times before asking, "Oh, I'm sorry to hear that. I didn't hear that you were leaving us."

Planning to not work your notice period was frowned upon, so Regina decided to sidestep that detail. "I wanted to pass along a presentation my assistant Arjun pulled together. He's got a very creative eye and the business acumen to go alongside it. I'm sure he's wasted working as a marketing assistant."

Sheila thought for a moment. "Arjun...Arjun...yes, I think I may have seen him around."

"He's very impressive," Regina explained. "I just wanted to speak with you before I sent his presentation over."

"I appreciate that. I'll definitely look it over," Sheila said. "But I'm very sad to hear you're leaving us."

"Yes, me too," Regina lied. "It just wasn't quite right for me."

"Well, we have to do what's best for ourselves," Sheila agreed. "All the best for the future."

"Thank you. You too."

Regina took the stairwell down to her office, firing off the pre-prepared email to Sheila as she went. She looked at the plain walls and reminded herself that it would be the last time she'd see them. Amandine would soon be a tiny blip in her life. Whatever came next, she could be sure that it wouldn't be Amandine.

She approached Arjun and gestured for him to join her in her office. Once they were out of the main office, she closed the door.

"I'm leaving," she told him. "As in right now."

"She fired you?" he asked.

"No, it's my choice."

Arjun looked relieved. "Good. I'm glad it's on your terms. And I'm glad you're getting away from her."

She patted his upper arm. "Thank you. I appreciate that. I sent your presentation straight to Sheila. She's promised me she'll look it over."

"Sheila?" Arjun's eyes widened in panic.

"Don't worry. It's a great presentation. You have good insight and wonderful ideas. I know that you'll do well."

Arjun looked so pleased he appeared taller as he puffed out his chest a little. "Thank you. It's been great working with you, even with everything. Where are you off to?"

"A highly risky start-up," Regina said.

Arjun laughed. "Sounds fun."

"It's actually pretty frightening," she confessed.

He shrugged. "Eh, what's the worst that can happen? No one can take away your birthday, right?"

She chuckled. "Let's hope not. Anyway, I better go before the word gets out that I'm going. Stay in touch, okay?"

"I will. Thanks again."

Regina grabbed her pen off the desk and looked one last time to check she'd left everything she needed to. She removed her pass from her pocket and laid it on top of her laptop. With a final breath of relief, she left her office for the last time.

In reception, she found Grace exactly where she'd left her a little over half an hour ago. Despite Regina's reassurances that she'd be absolutely fine, Grace had resolved to wait for her.

As she approached, she realised Grace was looking at one of the huge posters that adorned the walls of reception. It was a poster of Grace from a few years before. She was wearing a cocktail dress, holding a martini in one hand and a pair of heels in the other.

She stood beside Grace and looked up at the poster.

"Everything okay?"

Grace nodded, not taking her eyes off the poster. "Yes. I've decided I'm going to quit. Well, I'm going to put a date on my retirement." She looked at Regina. "Six months. It's not too far away, but not around the corner either. I can work on my remaining contracts and finish up some projects. But it means I leave on my own terms."

"If that's what you want to do," Regina said. "You know best."

Grace nodded. "I'll speak to my agent about it. It's time."

"New beginnings all round," Regina said.

"Did you do it?" Grace asked, shaken out of her own thoughts.

"I did. I think she might have even listened to me."

Grace took Regina's hand. "I hope so. But now we get to celebrate. Ice cream and wine, I think."

"It's half past nine in the morning," Regina said, chuckling.

"Tea and ice cream," Grace corrected. "We can toast. To both of us taking the plunge and starting a new life."

"I'll toast to that," Regina said, nipping in and placing a soft kiss on Grace's lips.

Epilogue

Regina sat down at the circular table and let out an exhausted sigh. She pulled off her heels and massaged the balls of her feet. It probably wasn't the done thing at a wedding, but it was eleven o'clock and she'd been on her feet all day. She'd thought a wedding of two people in their eighties would be a nice, quiet affair which would end around eight. How wrong she was.

"You must be Regina?" the woman at the next table asked. They were the only two people taking a seat, and they were definitely amongst the youngest people in the room.

"That's me." She smiled at the woman, assuming that this was someone from Leonard's side, a good bet considering eighty percent of the guestlist had been populated from Leonard's extensive friends list. What had started out as a small wedding that could easily be hosted in Calm Acres' library had turned into a huge function requiring a much larger venue. Regina was quite sure that Leonard had invited everyone he had ever come into contact with.

"I'm Pam, I was Leonard's PA many, many moons ago."

"He must have been fun to work with," Regina commented. She'd gotten to know the man well over the last year and was certain he was the nicest man anyone could ever meet. When Bess and he had announced their engagement, Regina couldn't have been happier.

"Oh yes! He was always making silly jokes. King of the so-called dad joke. He made every day at work a pleasure," Pam said.

"It was sad to see him go, but he'd earned that early retirement. Not that he ever slowed down."

"No. He does have incredible energy." Regina looked to the dance floor where Leonard was dancing with Grace.

"That's your partner, isn't it?" Pam asked.

"It is. Grace."

"She looks familiar, has she been on TV?"

"No. But she was a model," Regina said, a little pride creeping into her tone as it always did when she helped someone place exactly where they knew Grace. "Lots of fashion brands."

Pam snapped her fingers. "That's it. Yes. I think she's in the pictures at my gym."

Regina cast her mind back through Grace's work history. "Yes, she did some yoga clothing at one point."

"That's it." Pam nodded. "Must be interesting, dating a model."

"It was. I had no idea how much went into it," Regina said. The first six months of their relationship had been an education. Grace explained all the different brands she worked with and the different looks and feels they wanted, as well as the tricks of the trade. "She's retired now."

"Oh? So young."

"She's considered old in the modelling world," Regina said, rolling her eyes. "Still, she managed her own retirement, which was nice. She made the decision that she wanted to go and left on her own terms."

"That's good. Good on her. Ridiculous that anyone would think she's old. Look at her. It's a man's world, sometimes, isn't it?"

"It certainly is."

Bess arrived on Arjun's arm. "Hello poppet, hi Pam."

Regina pulled out a chair for her, and Arjun guided her towards it. As soon as she was settled she groaned a little. "Oh, thank you, love. It's nice to have a sit down."

"Pleasure, Mrs. Gibbs," Arjun said.

"Oh, it's going to take a while to get used to that," Bess said with a giggle.

Regina looked at her with a smile. She'd clearly had the very best of days. She knew weddings were supposed to be magical, perfect days, but in reality that was rarely the case. The event took over the people and became stressful and complicated. But this wedding was different. It had been designed to be exactly what Bess and Leonard wanted, with multiple people pitching in to make sure that everything was the way they wanted it.

"I think we're going to be heading off," Arjun said.

Bess took hold of his hand. "Thank you for coming. It was lovely having you here and lovely Maya, too."

"Thank you for inviting us," he said. He looked up at Regina and smiled cockily. "See you Monday, poppet."

She narrowed her eyes at him. "I'm regretting hiring you," she joked. "Remind me, you're still in your probationary period, right?"

"Three months in," he said.

Bess smacked her arm. "Don't tease him. He's wonderful."

Arjun grinned but wisely said nothing. " 'Night."

They waved him goodnight.

"How are you, Pam?" Bess asked. "Having a nice time?"

"Yes, it's been so nice, Bess. Such a lovely service."

Bess beamed.

Nick approached them. "Ladies. I'm coming to say goodnight."

Bess laughed. "These youngsters are falling like flies."

Nick bent down and kissed Bess's cheek. "We just don't have the stamina." He looked to Regina. "Let's grab a drink sometime. I'm in contact with this new robotics firm. Exciting stuff!"

"Sounds interesting, drop me a line," Regina said.

"I will." He headed back into the crowd.

"I thought you and he worked together?" Pam asked. "I thought that was what Leonard told me, anyway?"

"It went bust," Bess said. "You worked together for, what, seven months?"

Regina nodded. "Around that."

"Oh my," Pam said. "I'm sorry to hear that."

Regina smiled. "It was fun while it lasted, and it gave me some great career experience. I ended up in a similar company not long after. It's an interesting industry."

Bess rolled her eyes. "Don't ask about her about AI. We'll be here for days."

Pam chuckled.

"And then she hired young Arjun—isn't he a handsome fellow?" Bess added. "He was going to work in design but decided he missed marketing. I don't know what it is about marketing. Grace is getting into it, too."

Pam and Bess continued talking, but Regina's gaze was caught by Grace standing alone on the dance floor and beckoning for Regina to join her.

"Excuse me." She slipped on her shoes and joined Grace on the dance floor.

Grace draped her arms around Regina's neck. "This wedding is lovely."

"It is," Regina agreed.

"And long," Grace whispered.

Regina laughed. "I know, I was sure everyone would be in bed two hours ago."

"Leonard said it's because they've all saved their energy up for today," Grace said.

"Leonard has an endless supply of energy."

"True. But I do not," Grace said. "I'm looking forward to seeing our bed."

"Agreed." Regina placed a soft kiss on Grace's cheek. "Thank you for helping with everything today."

"Of course," Grace said. "It's been so much fun. And frankly anything to take my mind off the interview on Monday."

"You'll be fine," Regina reassured her.

"I hope so. I really want this job." Grace's expression darkened with nerves.

Regina picked up the pace of their dancing, spinning them around a couple of times to bring the smile back to Grace's face.

"What will be, will be," Regina said. It was a mantra that had slowly but surely replaced her old fears. She'd learned to not hold on too tightly to the status quo and to not worry so much about change. Sometimes change brought a negative, and sometimes it brought a positive, but worrying did little to impact the outcome.

She'd learned that freeing herself of fear and living in the moment was where true happiness lay.

About the Author

Amanda Radley had no desire to be a writer but accidentally turned into an award-winning, best-selling author. Residing in the UK with her wife and pets, she loves to travel. She gave up her marketing career in order to make stuff up for a living instead. She claims the similarities are startling.